Progressive Dinner Deadly

A Myrtle Clover Cozy Mystery, Volume 2

Elizabeth Spann Craig

Published by Elizabeth Craig, 2015.

PROGRESSIVE DINNER DEADLY

First edition. June 12, 2015.

Written by Elizabeth Spann Craig.

For Riley and Elizabeth Ruth with much love.

Chapter One

"The first step," said Myrtle to her friend Miles, "is to stage a coup."

Miles took off his wire rimmed glasses and rubbed his eyes. "A coup."

Myrtle beamed as if at a prize student. "That's it. The book club—as we know it—must be abolished."

"You're saying ... now stop me if I've got this wrong ... that you and I—the *new* members of the decades-old book club—will somehow commandeer it away from its current leadership, force it to restructure, and compel the members to read literature we deem worthy instead of beach books."

"That," said Myrtle, thumping *The Complete William Butler Yeats* triumphantly, "is exactly what I'm saying."

Miles looked at his friend. She was really on a roll this time—she'd run her hand through her poofy white hair until it stood up on end like Einstein's. She stood six feet tall, not at all bent or cowed by her considerable years.

"And you're proposing that we do this *how?*"

"It's a simple marketing principle. You're a former businessman, you must understand it. Marketing, you know. Delivering what the people need."

"Myrtle, I was an engineer, not a salesman." Myrtle shrugged. Miles gave a sigh. "And we're doing this *why?*"

Myrtle rolled her eyes. "You weren't listening again. We're doing this because book clubs should celebrate great literature. Literature, sharing a wonderful story, is what brings the world together. *Trixie Does Myrtle Beach* does not accomplish this goal."

Miles leaned forward in his chair. "Are you saying the book club actually picked a book called—"

"No, no. I'm saying that's the kind of tripe you might find on its reading list. And once we've started down that road?" She took a deep breath.

"The falcon cannot hear the falconer;
Things fall apart; the Centre cannot hold;
Mere anarchy is loosed upon the world."

Miles glanced over at the *Yeats* collection. "Got it." He straightened his glasses. "You believe that if we offer the book club serious reading alternatives, they'll follow us in droves. That we'll have taken it over. I'm just not sure it's going to work out that way. It seems a little too easy."

Myrtle snapped her fingers. "Good point. And I've got a terrific idea."

Miles groaned.

"If things *don't* go well, I need a plan B. I fully anticipate that everything will go according to plan, but if it doesn't, then I'll leave to go to the bathroom. And *you'll* say, "I think Myrtle has a great idea.""

"And why," asked Miles, pushing his wire-rimmed glasses up his nose, "would they care what I think?"

"Half those ninnies have set their cap for you, Miles. You're the new widower on the block, you know. Anything you say will be taken as gospel."

Miles looked doubtful at the appeal his steel-gray hair, wire-rimmed glasses, and seventy years held for the Bradley widows.

"Think of it Miles—you can still drive! You're a hot commodity for aging widows, I promise you. Here's our plan. I'll listen in from the hall and when they've decided it's a good idea, I'll come back in and get it all organized!" Myrtle was practically rubbing her hands together in glee.

"Don't count your chickens until they hatch," said Miles. "You never know how things could turn out."

"Nonsense. I predict we'll make a smooth transition to being a club with honest literary discussions."

"You know," said Miles, "no one else seems unhappy with the book club. You—a retired English teacher—are the only one needing honest literary discussions."

Myrtle shook her head impatiently. "Because they don't know what they're missing."

"Have you told Red that you're planning a literary coup?"

Myrtle just glowered at him.

"You haven't because you know he'll think you're just stirring up trouble again. Remember Red's motto? 'Leave well enough alone.'"

"That's only because my son is the police chief and wants me to live in stagnant misery so I can't cause him any trouble. I want to wake up the town of Bradley! Take their blinders off and show them the possibilities! And Red is fixed on keeping me out of his hair. Did you know that he signed me up for some volunteer work this weekend? The cheek."

"I'm assuming that's why the army of gnomes resides in your front yard?"

Myrtle put her extensive collection of ceramic gnomes on display for Red's viewing displeasure whenever he tried manipulating her. Lately, the gnomes had been on Myrtle's front lawn more often than not.

"That's exactly why the gnomes are out there. So he's already well aware that I'm displeased with him. I don't think he'll have a problem in the world with some reorganizing on my part."

"I don't know, Myrtle. I can't seem to shake this sinking feeling that our reorganization of the book club might have unexpected consequences."

Myrtle squinted at her rooster wall clock. Where was that blasted Puddin? She was supposed to have been dusting Myrtle's knickknacks hours ago. A phone call was in order. Myrtle steeled herself. Puddin never answered her calls—it was always her ancient husband, Dusty, Myrtle's yard man. Always assuming Myrtle was calling for him, he answered her greeting with some variation of, "It's too hot to mow!" Puddin wasn't exactly enchanting to talk to, but it beat Dusty howling at her like an old basset hound.

Myrtle dialed their number. The phone rang five or six times then, "Hullo?" asked a gruff voice.

Myrtle sighed. "Dusty? It's Mrs. Clover."

There was a great yowl on the other end. "Too wet to mow, Miz Clover!"

"For heaven's sake! It hasn't rained for days, Dusty. And that little teaspoon of water that trickled down evaporated before it even hit the clay."

"My blades'll get clogged. It'll empty smelly grass clods all over your yard, Miz Clover. And I saw them gnomes in your yard when I drove by. Them things is the dickens to cut around."

"Never mind. I wasn't calling for you, anyway. Your nonsense knocked me off track. May I speak to Puddin? She's supposed to be cleaning my house now."

Dusty hollered for Puddin and after a few minutes during which Myrtle wondered if she'd been hung up on, Puddin sullenly answered. Myrtle could imagine the dour expression on her face.

Before Myrtle could summon up a pleasant-enough voice to find out why Puddin was hanging out with Dusty instead of doing a mediocre job cleaning up Myrtle's house, Puddin muttered, "Back's thrown out, Miz Clover."

Myrtle bit her tongue. She did not need to have her "help" quit on her before she'd lined someone else up. But how convenient. Puddin's back always threw itself out whenever Puddin didn't want to polish silver, scrub dishes, or work at all.

"I haven't got time for your foolishness, Puddin. Book club is coming over tomorrow. Are you *sure* you just can't take an ibuprofen?"

Puddin considered this. "Hmm. No. It's thrown, all right."

Apparently the conversation was over because Puddin said, "Have a good club," and clunk! Myrtle heard a dial tone.

Myrtle pushed the receiver onto its base with unusual force. There was nothing to do but call in reinforcements. As irritating as Puddin's defection was, it was probably for the best.

Puddin was just not going to do for this Very Special book club meeting. Puddin, in her current state of unhelpfulness, was entirely inappropriate for a book club cleaning.

Extreme times called for extreme measures. Myrtle needed a cleaning A-team. She picked up the phone. Blanche Clark should have a good housekeeping recommendation. Considering Blanche lived in a sprawling chateau, she must have at least one person helping her clean, if not a small army.

As she made her call, she noticed a scrawny-looking black cat peering at her through the window. She'd seen the cat before—it was clearly a stray. It ran off, but she swore it had an approving look on its face as she dialed Blanche's phone number.

Jill, reflected Myrtle an hour later, was a top-notch cleaning sensation.

It was lucky, thought Myrtle as she watched Jill Caulfield's energetic cleaning, that she'd been able to get a substitute in such short order. The idea of pushing around dust and mopping her own floor had lost its appeal. But Jill was delighted at the opportunity and was certainly doing a great job. A member of Myrtle's book club, she seemed to have fallen on hard times. What was even nicer is that she lived right on Myrtle's street, just around the bend.

"Cleaning isn't *so* bad," said Jill as she expertly glossed Myrtle's end table with lemon oil until it shone. "I'm good at it. It's a steady job. It's good exercise."

"And," she continued as she buffed, "it's money in the bank." She briefly stopped her buffing and looked directly at Myrtle. "You know what I mean? Sometimes you just do what you have to do to survive in this world."

"Teaching preschool doesn't cover your bills, I'm guessing," said Myrtle, clucking.

"Not a bit. It helps, of course. But it's just not going to be enough for me and Cullen. And Cullen, with his disability and everything ... " Here she paused and searched Myrtle's face for any signs of disbelief. "Well, he just can't work. And that does make things tough. But I'll never leave him, Miss Myrtle. Not ever."

"I will never desert Mr. Micawber!" thought Myrtle, although Cullen Caulfield was no Mr. Micawber. His disability, well-known by all of Bradley, was his insatiable desire for alcohol.

Jill was now finished with the tables and, very sensibly adopting a top to bottom approach to cleaning, was cleaning the floors.

Myrtle said, "I'm just delighted you could help me out on such short notice. I'm too old to push around my own dust. I got your number from Blanche Clark. She'd been bragging on you during the last book club meeting, you know—how great you cleaned."

Jill suddenly became very focused on scrubbing a stubborn spot on the floor. "Is that right?"

"So," said Myrtle in a purring voice, "I was surprised to hear you weren't working for Blanche anymore. She gave me your number," (somewhat ungraciously), "but said y'all had gone your separate ways." Actually, Blanche had gotten so mad just talking about Jill that her voice trembled on the phone and she'd spat out Jill's name like she was trying to rid her mouth of something nasty. It was interesting enough to want to investigate.

"Business relationships don't *always* work out," said Jill in a careless voice. "But I'm sure ours will. Need me to come by next week?"

Myrtle opened her mouth to say that Puddin would be there next week. But then *some*thing ... could it be the fresh clean pine scent? The gleaming tables? The attentive housekeeper in front of her? ... changed her mind. "I do believe I *will* have you over next week."

That darned Puddin never cleaned like this. She didn't have a *passion* for cleaning. Myrtle quieted the voice in her head that reminded her that Puddin and Dusty were a package deal—and *what* was she going to do without a yardman? Even a very *bad* yardman?

"If you're okay here, Jill, I'm going to pop across the street to Elaine and Red's house for a little visit."

"I'll be fine. I saw Elaine the other day, but haven't seen Red for a while. How's he doing?"

"Oh. He's keeping the peace," said Myrtle with a shrug. The annoying thing was Myrtle's police chief son's insistence on keeping *her* peaceful. He interfered. "I'm really going over to get some cuddle time in with my grandson, Jack. He's got the cutest chubby legs ... " and she pulled out a handy album to prove it.

To her credit, Jill appeared thrilled to coo over grandbaby pictures. In fact, Jill was quite disgustingly perfect in every way. Puddin's sole redeeming quality was her quirkiness. Everything about Puddin was unknown: would she be in a chatty mood and yak at the kitchen table with you instead of cleaning? Would she have a nicotine fit and spend the entire morning smoking furiously outside? Would she show up for work at all?

Jill's perfection was enough to make Myrtle pine for the wicked Puddin. Almost.

Myrtle grabbed her cane from next to the front door and tapped her way down the front walk. There were a few birds perching on the gnomes that scattered, chirping, as she approached. She paused for a moment to survey her handiwork. Lots of little gnome backs were facing her since, of course, they were all arranged to maximize Red's viewing pleasure ... and passing motorists'. She chuckled, but the laugh turned into a gasp when a dreaded voice behind her asked nasally, "Fighting with Red again, I see?"

It was Erma Sherman ... her evil next door neighbor. Ordinarily, Myrtle carefully checked to make sure the coast was clear before venturing out her front door. Having her house restored to such an immaculate state had clearly made her giddy. As she saw Erma looming over her, arms outstretched for a determined hug, Myrtle reflected how fast one's mood could plummet.

"Just trying to make a subtle point," said Myrtle. Not that Erma would know the definition of the word *subtle*. "Red mistakenly thought it would be a good idea to volunteer me for the Kiwanis club pancake breakfast." Red frequently displayed this shockingly poor judgment. It was an appalling characteristic for a police chief to have.

"How will Dusty cut the grass around the gnomes?" asked Erma, looking pointedly at the spires of grass brushing the gnomes' bellies. "With a weed whacker?"

As if Dusty would own sophisticated yard equipment like weed whackers. "No, I guess he'll just cut what he can reach."

"How long are you planning to feud with Red?" asked Erma, frowning at Myrtle's grass and at a particularly animated gnome who seemed to be gleefully imbibing a beverage.

"How long are you planning to allow your crabgrass to infest my yard?"

Erma gaped at Myrtle, then erupted with haw-haws of laughter. "Don't you have that backwards, Myrtle? There's a whole crop of crabgrass right there that looks like you've actually been fertilizing it."

There was, actually, quite a bare spot there that Erma's weeds had made inroads with. She'd shoot that Dusty! She'd *asked* him to aerate and seed.

Myrtle turned toward the street when she heard a gentle toot-toot of a car horn. It was her daughter-in-law Elaine, waving out her minivan window and looking sympathetically at her. There went her whole reason for being outside to begin with. "I've got to go in," she gritted out between her teeth.

"But you were coming out for a reason, Myrtle. Can't you remember what it is? Let's see, you were heading out here, without your bag. You weren't planning on going very far, were you? Let's retrace your steps." Erma also displayed sympathy, but it was a more salacious version that would likely be spread all over town: "Did you hear? Myrtle Clover has gone completely gaga! Couldn't even remember why she'd left the house yesterday!" "Oh, what a shame!"

Myrtle spun around and thumped back up the walkway. "Have a good one, Myrtle. See you at book club tomorrow!" called Erma behind her.

Not if I see you first, thought Myrtle. She slipped quickly into her front door and leaned against it. Next time she'd be more careful when she ventured outside. She listened for the sound of Jill in the kitchen, but didn't hear anything. No sounds of cleaning at all. Curious, she walked through the kitchen to the back of the house.

When she peered through her bedroom door, she saw the light on in the bathroom. She hadn't meant Jill to waste any time cleaning in there since it was still pretty clean from the week before. She walked back to the bathroom.

There she saw Jill, face obscured by the medicine cabinet door. There were several bottles of pills on the sink and a couple of other bottles in her hand. Myrtle tiptoed back to the front of the house. Why was Jill rooting around in her medicines? Was she a prescription drug addict? No, Jill was too clear-headed, too detail-oriented with her cleaning. She seemed a lot less befuddled than Puddin did. Maybe she sold prescription drugs on the black market? There had been an article in the newspaper recently about drugs being sold on the internet at rock bottom prices. Could it be yet another way for Jill to make extra money?

Myrtle slipped out the front door and then noisily re-entered. By the time she'd thumped back into the kitchen, Jill was busily cleaning in there. "Elaine wasn't home, so I'll have to catch up with her later. Instead, I ran into Erma Sherman," Myrtle couldn't repress a shudder. "Otherwise known as the neighbor from hell."

Jill laughed. "Is she that bad? I've always kind of liked her when I've seen her at book club, but I don't have to live next to her. But I noticed she didn't take care of her yard. I'm such a stickler about the yard, it would drive me nuts to have crabgrass creeping over the border."

"You must be a good neighbor to have, then," said Myrtle in a wistful voice. Aside from the possibility she'd sneak in your house and searching through your stuff, of course.

"Oh, I have a lot of fun with the house. The yard is one of my hobbies, I guess."

When the heck did Jill Caulfield find time for a hobby? Between two jobs, volunteering at church, and trying to keep her husband out of trouble, she must be pretty busy.

"When I think about your yard, Jill, I think about all those Christmas lights you string up every year." Myrtle was careful to smile. No need to have Jill realize that her Christmas extravaganza didn't put Myrtle in the holiday spirit. In fact, Jill's decorations made Myrtle quite Grinchy. How many times had she nearly been mowed down by a creeping car whose occupants were gorging their eyes on neon Santas and twelve foot nutcrackers with ominous grins? On top of that was the music— *Holly, Jolly Christmas* and some other annoying tunes on a loop blasting from speakers from November fifteenth through January fifth.

Jill smiled. "So many people have told me the same thing, Miss Myrtle. They look forward all year to our light and music show. It's just not Christmas for them until they drive past our house, they say."

"Do the lights and music go on all night?" Myrtle was scandalized. This was definitely cause to revise her thoughts on Jill's suitability as a next-door neighbor. "I can't see your house from here since it's right around the bend in the road."

"Only from five to midnight. Everyone is simply crazy over it. They've told me our display is such a blessing. Jill, they say, when the *Twelve Days of Christmas* starts playing, we get tears in our eyes."

Especially Sherry Angevine next door, guessed Myrtle. "So you string all these lights and speakers and things up yourself? Doesn't Cullen help you?" That dog.

Jill suddenly glowed with an almost spiritual, evangelistic radiance. "Not with his disability. He couldn't, could he? No, I'm *honored* to put them up for him. Really. Then he has a Merry Christmas and doesn't have to worry about the decorating."

She clearly loved this Jill-the-Martyr act. Myrtle said, "Would you like some sweet tea, Jill? I think I need something sugary to bolster me after my encounter with my next door monster."

"No thanks, Miss Myrtle. I'm getting ready to finish up. I'll see myself out, okay? And then I'll be back tomorrow for the club meeting. Did you read the book?" Myrtle looked at Jill blankly. "*Jennifer's Promise*? Remember?"

Myrtle's skin prickled with irritation at the thought of subjecting herself to *Jennifer's Promise*. "No. No, I didn't get around to it, Jill."

"Well, don't worry about it, dear. These books get so complicated. I only read the first few pages, myself. I wish they'd choose a really quick read—you know?"

Clearly Jill was not going to be on the side of great literature during the book club coup. Myrtle took her tea into the living room to think a little more about Jill. She wouldn't just have been in her medicine cabinet for an aspirin. No, she was after something. Not that she'd found it there. The cabinet was crammed with ancient amoxicillin bottles, dated over-the-counters, some blood pressure meds, and an old bottle of witch hazel.

Was Jill's snooping the reason Blanche Clark fired her? Did Jill discover something about Blanche that made it impossible for her to keep her on?

When book club morning dawned, Myrtle climbed out of bed with high hopes. Minutes later, she was already devising what novels might be a good introduction into the world of books. Because, Myrtle thought, the stuff that the book club had been focusing on definitely couldn't qualify as books.

Milton *might* be a little ambitious for the group, she admitted as she boiled grits and threw in a liberal amount of butter into the spitting, spattering mixture. Dickens would be an easy adjustment. Everyone was familiar with his books anyway and it would be a popular place to start. Yes, maybe *David Copperfield* instead of *Paradise Lost*. Milton's masterpiece was too richly worded—book club might get ill on the richness of the imagery after starving themselves on beach rot for years.

Hours later at the meeting, though, Myrtle had given up hope of proposing Dickens as a book club selection. The coup was not going well. Everything had actually started out just fine with the ladies trickling into Myrtle's living room like little lambs and lining up sweetly for their muffins, cookies, and iced tea. Both Blanche Clark and Jill Caulfield were there and successfully keeping apart from each other. The entire book club membership was actually very well represented, considering it was late summer and prime traveling time. There were about fifteen ladies in Myrtle's living room and kitchen.

Miles stood next to Myrtle's fireplace, looking uneasy. He clutched a copy of *Absalom! Absalom!* and fingered the knickknacks on the mantle. Myrtle had cleverly designed new end tables by several of the chairs by stacking large books from her personal library on top of each other. Each book was a masterpiece, of course. "What a fun idea, Myrtle!" chirped one of the ladies. Myrtle beamed. If the members were *surrounded* with excellent literature, Myrtle knew they wouldn't be able to resist.

Finally Tippy Chambers, the well-heeled club president, called the meeting to order. After the minutes to the last meeting were read (Tippy being a stickler for Parliamentary Procedure, even for a book club), She asked if there were any new business. Myrtle straightened in her chair, then rose carefully to her feet. She noticed that, like a seesaw, when she stood up, Miles sank down into a chair. He looked pasty white and a bit of perspiration trickled down the side of his head. How *had* he survived the dog eat dog world of business?

Myrtle cleared her throat and used her best retired-teacher voice. Even after all these years of retirement, it still had a weighty pitch that carried to the corners of the room. The right kind of voice to make an important announcement.

"I've been thinking," she intoned, "about ways to improve our book club. What has brought us together is our mutual love for literature." There were nods of agreement and Myrtle soldiered on, taking a deep breath.

"But I don't think that the books we're been focusing on," here she lifted up a copy of *Jennifer's Promise* in illustration, "are worthy recipients of our leisure time. I think," Myrtle said sternly, "that our time could be better spent."

There was a small pause. Then Erma Sherman piped up, bobbing her head emphatically. "You know, I was thinking the same thing, Myrtle." Myrtle doubted it. "The books we're picking only take a little bit of the meeting to review."

There was a chorus of agreement.

Myrtle said quickly, "So what I was thinking ... " she bent to reach for a handy volume of Charles Dickens.

Erma jumped in again from the floor. Why did Tippy's Parliamentary order nonsense never occur when it needed to? "So why don't we change the club?" she demanded loudly. She was warming up to the subject and seemed to be on a roll. "Instead of reading books, we could turn it into a ... supper club!"

There were oohs of agreement and stomach rumblings among the ladies. Even Tippy was caught up in the fervor. "We could," she suggested, "make it a progressive dinner supper club. You know—one house for the drinks and appetizers, another for soups and salads, a third for the main course, and dessert at the end."

Now the room was buzzing. "That way it wouldn't be too much for just one person!" said Jill Caulfield.

"Our husbands could even participate in it," said Blanche.

Erma proudly surveyed the room, which had become electrified with her idea. Myrtle stood there, open-mouthed, clutching Dickens. Miles looked torn between amusement and horror. What would he care? thought Myrtle viciously. He was a foodie just as much as a reader. It would work out well for him no matter what.

It was time to abort this plan and head into Emergency Plan B. Myrtle rose abruptly and walked toward the hall. She looked behind her. Her entire library was animated with discussion and Miles just soaked it all in.

Myrtle cleared her throat. But Miles was absorbed in watching Erma. He had a revolted expression on his face as she blathered on, off-topic as usual, about her cousin who shot deer and stored the carcasses, whole, in a huge freezer in his garage. Myrtle again cleared her throat and walked, exaggeratedly, toward the bathroom. No response from Miles.

"I *think*," said Myrtle in her former-schoolteacher voice, which had the power to silence the room, "I will go to the bathroom!" She glared at Miles, who looked flustered.

Tippy looked concerned. "Are you sick, Myrtle?"

"No. I just think I'll go to the bathroom."

"Well," said Tippy in a puzzled tone, "of course. Anyone is free to visit the restroom at any time."

The room remained quiet until Myrtle was out of sight. Then Erma said, "No wonder she's feeling sick! She's the worst cook in the history of the world. She probably ate some of her own chicken salad sandwiches." Erma pointed to indicate the full and untouched platter of sandwiches.

"Good point," said Tippy in a low voice. "Does anyone know if Myrtle made the chicken salad or bought it?"

Myrtle listened, fuming, in the hall. "Although her chicken salad is *excellent*, I know for a fact that she ran low on time and purchased this batch," Miles said. His voice sounded pained.

Myrtle peeped around the side of the door. The women looked at Miles curiously as there was suddenly a run on the chicken salad sandwiches.

"And while we're talking about Myrtle," said Miles, in was apparently a desperate attempt to wrestle the wayward conversation back on track, "I think she had an excellent idea."

"I do too," said Tippy warmly. "It was so clever of her to think up a supper club. She was absolutely right that book club was getting stale."

Myrtle gritted her teeth.

"I meant her suggestion that the book club start reading some different kinds of books." Miles tugged at his collar.

"Was that her idea?" Tippy sounded dubious. "Well, her supper club idea is much sounder."

"Now if we can only convince her not to cook!" said Erma. She gave a sneering laugh.

Jill Caulfield said, "I've got a great recipe for pulled pork for the slow cooker. How about if I cook the main course for our first supper club?"

The room was soon buzzing again with ideas for how the supper club would run, who would provide what, and who would host the various courses. Sullenly, Myrtle came back in and sat down with the others. She drummed her fingers on her copy of *The Sound and the Fury* as Tippy efficiently organized the details of the supper club. Miles offered to host the hors d'oeuvres and drinks. There was a clamoring over different recipes and whether they should have a theme for each event.

Myrtle replayed the last few minutes in her head. Everything had gone wrong when Erma had piped up. She instinctively seemed to know what to do to mess up Myrtle's plans.

Myrtle straightened up in her chair. She wouldn't let it happen. She was going to regain control of this meeting. "Actually," she said in a booming voice. "I had another idea completely. We could certainly have a *parallel* club that meets for suppers. But giving up on book club just because the selection has been weak … "

Amazingly, Erma stepped in again. "Weak is right," she agreed. "I never did get what the writer was trying to say with that Bo and the Boy Scout book we did that one time."

Myrtle said through gritted teeth, "You mean *To Kill a Mockingbird.*"

"Which you'd *think* would be about endangered birds! When I read, I want to be able to understand the point! But there aren't enough books like *Jennifer's Promise*, so we end up reading about Boy Scouts. But food … we all understand food."

Myrtle stared at Erma's protruding tummy and figured that some people understood it better than others. She opened her mouth again to explain that *To Kill a Mockingbird* was real literature and that there were many others where that came from—but then snapped her mouth shut again. Because where would she start with that argument? How could you argue with someone as dense as Erma Sherman? "Mockingbirds are *not* endangered," was all she could muster.

Tippy Chambers pushed a strand of blonde hair off her forehead. "I think the point really is," she said, "that we've been doing book club for a long time and we're ready for a change. A supper club would be fun, and we can even get our husbands involved." Myrtle opened her mouth to argue and Tippy injected quickly, "Would you be interested in having the desserts at your house, Myrtle? I remember your blackberry cobbler was the best I'd ever had."

Myrtle puffed up a little in her chair. Miles smiled. Diplomacy was the reason why Tippy was the perfect president of anything. Miles clearly recalled Myrtle's blackberry cobbler as a soggy, undercooked disaster. But Myrtle was already planning her dessert menu, happily putting the unkind comments about her cooking out of her head.

"Y'all, I've got to run," said Jill Caulfield, picking up her pocketbook. "I've got a house to clean. So I'll host the main course, and we said two weeks from today? I'll have it all set up."

When Jill walked out, Tippy said quickly, "I'm a little concerned about Jill having to provide all the food for the main course. I think that's ... well, it's a lot to ask."

"Why *did* she offer to provide the main course?" Miles quietly asked Myrtle. "Didn't you say that Jill just cleaned your house? Providing a barbeque dinner for a house full of people is kind of a pricy proposition, isn't it?"

Myrtle murmured, "I strongly suspect that Jill likes everyone to feel sorry for her. She piles that misery on herself. You know, the whole 'Poor Jill' thing. But she sure does know how to clean a house. I'm going to ditch that Puddin of mine."

"There will probably be thirty people there, if we include spouses," Tippy was saying. "Are there three or four people who can volunteer to bring some sides in?"

A few hands went up. At the same time, the front door opened and Jill's sister Willow came in. The hands drooped, and then fell under the censorious eye of Tippy. No one wanted to mention Jill's financial situation. Especially around Willow, who was sure to blame her brother-in-law for any money problems her sister might face.

Willow's long, prematurely-gray hair swung around her shoulders. With her hair down, her black tunic over a long, ruffled black skirt, and the amulet around her neck, Willow looked like she'd escaped from a coven.

"Sorry I'm late," she said in her low, sing-song voice. "Was that Jill I saw pulling out?"

Erma nodded, eyes dancing as she anticipated trouble. "Yes it was. She was off to clean somebody's house."

Willow's face darkened.

Tippy jumped in with a quelling look at Erma. "We're all hearing wonderful things about Jill's housekeeping. It seems that she has a wonderful talent for hearth and home."

Myrtle glanced quickly over at Blanche, who grimaced before her face resumed its usual placid mask.

Willow shook her head and fingered her amulet. "All this work isn't good for her. She's got two really draining jobs. She should be reconnecting with her spirit instead of scrubbing people's bathrooms."

Erma nodded sympathetically, avoiding Tippy's quelling glare. "Which she could do if Cullen could go back to work. Such a shame about his *disability* and all," said Erma, who sounded hopeful for some disability details, which Willow seemed unwilling to elaborate on. "But don't worry. Even though Myrtle changed the book club into a supper club, and Jill took the main course, we're all going to chip in with the sides so Jill can afford to host it."

Tippy jumped in again in her continuing effort to keep control of the meeting. "Willow. I'd better fill you in. Myrtle suggested we change the book club to a supper club." Myrtle clenched her teeth. "We're starting it two weeks from today. Miles will have the hors d'oeuvres and drinks, Jill's covering the main course, and Myrtle is hosting the dessert."

Willow thought a moment. "What if I host a soup or salad course? It'll keep the progressive dinner moving."

"Great idea," said Tippy. "That cements our plan for the first progressive dinner. The best part is that y'all all live on the same street; we can easily walk from the appetizers to the salads, to the main course, to the dessert. And maybe even enjoy a little wine along the way!" Tippy gave her tinkling laugh. "And thanks again to Myrtle for her brainstorm. To Myrtle!" she said, raising a glass of sweet tea.

"To Myrtle!" everyone chimed in, holding their tea aloft.

Myrtle was ready to trade in her sweet tea for something a bit stronger.

Chapter Two

Jill's cat, Miss Chivis, was busily pooping in next door neighbor Sherry Angevine's yard. Sherry glared out the window as Miss Chivis scratched up a big pile of pine needles to semi-cover her transgression. Sherry wondered how many times Jill's cat or dog had pooped in her yard while she'd been at book club. It was yet another reason to hate Jill Caulfield.

There were actually many, many reasons to hate Jill. The leaf blower that blared *every* Saturday morning and many Sundays. The oh-so-perfect flower beds with just the right color combinations of impatiens or pansies. The five million Christmas lights that went up two weeks before Thanksgiving and came down two weeks after Christmas and lit up the neighborhood like a carnival.

But Sherry had found a way to funnel her anger against Jill and get revenge on her at exactly the same time. She had a secret.

Willow let herself into her house and sat down on a corner of a sofa draped with six different cats, all in various stages of napping. There were eight more felines in other parts of the house and a couple of feral cat families that used her backyard as a home base. All five of the dogs came barreling up to greet her and she absently scratched them behind the ears.

Willow had consulted the stars and read her tea leaves, but hadn't yet found any answers to her problem. How could she get her sister to leave Cullen Caulfield? Jill was wasting her life with Cullen. Willow thought about Jill's volunteer work and how much *more* she could do if she didn't have Cullen drinking through all the money she scrabbled together. He treated his body like a sewer and just poured in that poison all day long.

Willow knew how he treated Jill, too. He yelled at her and belittled her and acted like her sole purpose in life was to wait on him hand and foot. And now Jill had invited over half the town of Bradley, North Carolina, to show off their dysfunctional household?

Cullen would probably drink for hours leading up to the party. And he wasn't one to stay hidden in the back of the house, either. No, he'd be right in with everyone else—laughing too loud, falling over things, knocking glasses over and yelling at his wife. Unless Willow found a way to stop him.

Blanche arrived home, totally drained from book club. This supper club was going to be a disaster. Now, instead of spending an hour and a half with Jill Caulfield, she was going to have to spend ... what? Three or four hours with her? It was intolerable, she thought, as she slipped on designer label sweats and started walking on her treadmill.

But what excuse could Blanche possibly give for getting out of it? Maybe it would have been better if she'd volunteered to host it herself. There was a lot more room in her own house to avoid Jill than in Jill's cramped bungalow with her alcoholic husband. And how was she going to survive another gathering where Saint Jill's praises were lauded? Book club had been bad enough with Tippy spouting off about Jill's cleaning prowess.

There was really no way to avoid this supper club. It was Bradley, after all: a small town. Escaping Jill Caulfield wasn't a long-term option. Unless something changed, Jill would remain an annoying thorn in her side. Blanche could only hope something would happen to Jill. If only she would disappear ...

Georgia was glad Jill was hosting supper club. She'd never be invited to Jill's house any other way. This could give her an opportunity to stab Jill in the back a few times. She imagined herself now: *Well, it is good barbeque. But I'd rather be a good person instead of a good cook.* Maybe she could put a sticky note in Jill's bathroom, saying what a pill Jill was. People were always saying, "Poor Jill! Taking care of that no-good husband and working two jobs!" But Georgia knew the truth about Jill. And she was ready to share it with everybody she knew.

Simon Caulfield said, "Excuse me? Jill is hosting a supper club at her house? For *how* many people?"

His wife, Libba, shrugged. "I'm guessing thirty or forty? There are usually about fifteen of us who make it to book club and then you count the spouses in there ... well, it'll be a big group."

"And she volunteered to host the main course? That's nuts! She cleans houses, for Pete's sake. She cleans *our* house sometimes."

Libba shook her head in frustration. "I'd rather she *didn't* though. Sometimes I get a funny feeling about her. And we really can't afford the help."

Simon said, "You need the help with the housework, Libba. Especially if the cancer is coming out of remission. While we can still afford the help, we need to get it for you."

Libba was no fan of Jill's, but felt the need to point out, "Jill is only cleaning houses because your brother can't hold down a job. The dinner won't be as big of a splurge as it sounds—several of the members are bringing sides. But I don't want to go. Cullen is so embarrassing. He'll probably be staggering around drunk the whole time. Can we stay at home?"

"No. I think we need to go and make sure Cullen doesn't make a fool of himself and embarrass us even *more*."

Libba picked off the last bit of pink nail polish that she'd only just painted on that morning.

Chapter Three

"I don't want to go tonight," said Myrtle, feeling stubborn.

"Oh come on, Myrtle. It won't be that bad," said Miles. "Every one of these folks is a great cook. You know all the people going. It'll be something fun and different. Besides—you're hosting the dessert. You've got to go."

"It'll be tedious and tiring. And I don't care about food as much as you do. I could just sit at home and wait for the club to get to my house. I'll sip sherry and read thoughtful books and grieve over my failed plan to transform that pitiful book club into something great."

"You're not even a little curious how Jill and Blanche are going to interact with each other at a party? I thought you'd wanted to get to the bottom of their feud."

Myrtle perked up. "It's a one-sided feud, that's the thing. Usually you've got two people upset with each other. But Jill seems just as pleased as punch when I bring up Blanche's name." She fiddled with the phone cord. "Okay, I'll be there. But don't be surprised if I leave early and go back home to wait for the dessert course."

Myrtle hung up and sighed. She still hadn't figured out exactly what she was going to do about these desserts she was supposed to cook for the progressive dinner. Myrtle wanted some fresh ideas and those old cookbooks of hers seemed really stale. She checked her watch. Shoot. The *Bradley Bugle's* editor, Sloan, had scheduled a meeting with her and she was running behind.

Myrtle's son Red had, over a year ago, gotten her hired to write a helpful hints column for the newspaper. He'd seemed to find it an appropriate activity for a retired English teacher with rather too much time on her hands. She'd been furious with Red at the time for meddling in her business. But she'd gotten so she liked writing the column, even if the tips that came in were fairly flaky. There were lots of superstitious people and old wives in Bradley, if their tips were anything to judge by.

Myrtle pushed open the old wooden door to the newsroom. The whole room smelled like ink, paper, and musty books. It was dimly lit and every corner was crammed with stacks of papers and photographs. It was, thought Myrtle with satisfaction, a wonderful place.

Sloan, a hefty man with an ever-expanding forehead and a busy demeanor, lifted his head as the door opened. "Miss Myrtle," he said, standing quickly.

Myrtle wondered if Sloan would ever lose that deferential manner toward her. She'd taught him in middle school and he obviously clearly remembered the tongue-lashings she'd given him and Red both as they'd rolled spitballs, passed notes, and thrown balls of paper around the classroom. Sloan and Red were both in their forties and those days were long gone, but the memory, apparently, lived on. Plus the fact that Myrtle, even in her eighties, could straighten up to an intimidating six feet when she wanted to.

"Thanks for coming over," said Sloan with one eye—as usual—on the clock. "I'm trying to expand the paper's readership a little bit. Many people don't subscribe anymore."

Myrtle frowned. She thought everybody subscribed to the *Bradley Bugle*. How else would they know what was going on?

"And your helpful hints column has gotten pretty popular. I know we get more tips in a week than we have space to put in the paper. So I thought you could put the extras on the *Bradley Bugle*'s blog."

"What? I didn't know the *Bugle* even had a blog."

"Well, we didn't until a few days ago. But I've been checking into it and it seems like a smart direction to take the paper in.

The next generation is almost definitely going to be getting their news online. I can have a mobile version for folks to read it easier on their phones. And the blog will have little extras that we don't have space for or the money to print in the paper version."

Myrtle wasn't sure exactly how to blog. But being an octogenarian blogger was an idea that definitely had legs to it. The idea of conquering technology, at her age, gave her a warm, smug feeling.

"I was even thinking," said Sloan, warming up to his subject, "that we could run a story on that supper club you're in."

"The progressive dinner thing?" asked Myrtle with surprise. "That's news?"

"It might not be interesting for expensive *newsprint* news," explained Sloan. "But it's perfect for online. You can mention the names of all the people who were there, the food that was served. Take some pictures and upload them. And then all those people will go online to read about themselves. You know how people are in Bradley. So you could play up the angle, butter them all up a little bit. And I'll have links on the blog site to subscribe to the paper. I think I've even got some local advertisers interested."

Myrtle still wasn't sold on the news value of the impending supper club that she hadn't been excited about to begin with. "Wellll. I guess so. I'm still trying to work out what to cook for it. I'm hosting desserts at my house and I want to try something different."

Sloan brightened. "You know what you could do? Check out the food blogs. There are tons of sites with recipes—and they even do step-by-step pictures on how to cook them. I use them a lot, living by myself. What do I know about cooking?"

Myrtle beamed. "Smart boy. Now *that's* a great idea." She bestowed on him one of her fondest looks, usually reserved for her grandson.

Sloan looked concerned that he might end up the unwilling recipient of a hug. He moved backwards a few steps. "Well good.

And thanks for the coverage on the progressive dinner. I think we're on to something really good."

After spending an hour studying food blogs, Myrtle was well and truly overwhelmed. She'd visited a couple of blogs before, but she'd had no clue that there were so many of them out there. And they all linked to each other, so when you went to one food blog, you discovered fifteen or twenty others that sounded good. She decided the food blog idea still sounded like a great source for recipes, but it wouldn't work out on such short notice. Myrtle walked over to the Piggly Wiggly, grabbed a couple of Key Lime pies and two dozen cupcakes and called herself done.

But she was still stuck cooking that side dish for Jill's part of the dinner, since she'd so shortsightedly volunteered to help out. Luckily, she cooked a mean three bean salad. She charged into the kitchen, full of confidence and good intentions.

Sadly, it did end up slightly overcooked, but that's because she was writing that darned blog post for Sloan and trying to figure out how to log on. He'd given her an instructions sheet to follow, but it wasn't as easy as he'd made out. The cheese on top of her casserole had gotten just a *little* bit singed. It was going to have to do, though—it was time for the dinner to start and she still had to hand off the side to Jill.

Myrtle wrapped the hot dish tightly in aluminum foil, carried it to Jill's house with her rooster oven mitts, and handed it off to the grateful Jill with relief. "See you in a few minutes, Miss Myrtle. I'm just putting the finishing touches on the baked beans. Y'all are so sweet to bring side dishes. Everybody has been so thoughtful."

"No problem, sweetie. And everything smells divine. See you in a few."

The problem with hosting a supper club was that most of the houses on the street were modest in size. Oh the houses definitely had their strong points; after all, they were on the lake and each one on Myrtle's side of the street had a dock with a boat. But the houses themselves were older homes, built in the 1950s. Most were your basic three-bedroom, two bathroom ranches. Miles had only two bedrooms and one bathroom. Which, Myrtle thought as she visited with Miles, was absolutely fine. All the space in the *world* that a bachelor needed. Except when hosting a supper club of thirty people. And especially when you provided them with alcohol, as Miles had so thoughtfully done for the hors d'oeuvres and cocktail leg of their culinary journey.

A booming belly-laugh erupted just feet away from them. Miles looked startled. "What was that?" he breathed.

"Georgia Simpson," said Myrtle. She frowned. "I wonder what she's doing here. She's isn't a reader. She wouldn't have even been in book club. And it *looks* like she's been drinking. I mean *seriously* drinking. With effort."

"Tippy called all the hosts to tell us to add one more person to the guest list. Apparently someone was interested in a supper club, but not a book club. I guess it must have been Georgia."

"So now we've reached a new club low," growled Myrtle.

The woman threw back her head and laughed her booming laugh again.

"The epitome of genteel Bradley womanhood. Stinking drunk in acquaintances' houses," muttered Miles.

"Keep it up, Miles. Don't think she won't hit a guy who wears glasses."

Miles looked somewhat affronted at this attack on his manhood.

Georgia embodied the idea of a tough cookie, from her big hair that never moved even in high winds, to the tattoos covering her arms and legs. Her eyelashes were so heavily encrusted with mascara that her eyes stayed permanently at half-mast, giving her a kind of glowering look. She had plucked out most of her eyebrows, the better to draw in a pair in whatever theme her expression-of-the-day was in. Her hair was black on the bottom with a white-blond layer on the top. She was fond of wearing tee-shirts that sported rude sayings. Myrtle nudged Miles with her foot. "You're gaping."

"She looks like a guy I was in Vietnam with," murmured Miles in wonder as Georgia strutted over to them and grunted a greeting.

"You know what this party needs?" Georgia asked in a grating voice.

Miles stopped gaping and managed a look of polite interest.

"Port-a-johns. You coulda had a couple put into your backyard, you know. Nice place, but one bathroom?"

Miles nodded eagerly in agreement. Myrtle rolled her eyes. "Miles lives by himself, Georgia. Why would he need more than one bathroom?"

But Georgia was already walking away. "Got to find a bathroom."

Myrtle looked after her, thoughtfully. "That's the best mood I've seen Georgia in for a while. Parties must agree with her."

"You *know* this person?" asked Miles. He had an awe-struck note in his voice. "You—the Charles Dickens and William Butler Yeats fan. You know this Georgia creature."

Myrtle looked at him as though he were addled. "Of course, Miles. I taught her."

"Taught her!"

"Miles, when you're as old as I am and taught for as long as I did, you've taught everybody in the town between the ages of thirty-five and sixty."

Jill quickly joined the line behind them, peering around Myrtle at Georgia's retreating back. This was interesting—*Jill* actually avoiding someone.

Myrtle hoped Miles didn't have anything in his medicine cabinet that he wanted to keep private.

"Dear God," breathed Miles, "there goes the party."

Myrtle craned her neck to see the front door. The inaptly-named Tiny, his looming figure filling the door frame, looked apprehensively into the room.

"What is *he* doing here?" wondered Myrtle. "He's no book club member. Or book club spouse. I'm not actually sure he's a reader at all."

"He's probably looking for a mate," said Miles. He gloomily took a swig of his cocktail. "Now that he's single again he's out on the town looking for a new wife to torment."

"Was he *ever* tiny?" mused Myrtle. "I can't actually remember a time that he was."

Tiny, by this time, had crammed his bulk into Miles's living room. He'd managed to squeeze his six foot seven, three hundred pound frame into an uncomfortable-looking, shiny suit. And, somehow, had forgotten his socks.

"Maybe it's his *brain* that's tiny?" murmured Miles.

"I'm surprised at you, Miles. That wasn't very nice."

"If *he* were nice, I wouldn't have said it."

"He always seems to smell like gasoline," mused Myrtle.

"Maybe after he's finished doing yard work he splashes a little on. Gasoline is just about as expensive as cologne these days, after all."

They watched as Tiny plowed through to the cocktail table. Miles watched him with glum eyes. "If I were going to have a gatecrasher, why couldn't it be someone else?"

Proving him right, Tiny immediately launched into an argument with Simon Caulfield and Georgia, who'd returned to the group—"There ain't nothing *wrong* with hunting, Simon."

"Guns are dangerous things," said Simon in an uptight voice, "I wouldn't dream of having one in my house. If you're a parent, which you are, you should be more responsible."

Tiny looked at Simon blankly at the mention of offspring. Then he recollected, "Oh. Well, he's eighteen, you know. No bitty guy ... "

Miles groaned. "This evening is a disaster. I've got Tiny Kirk party crashing and starting arguments and I'm not big enough to kick him out. I've got Georgia Simpson staggering around in search of portable toilets." He gestured at Georgia, who had a hand on Tiny's bulging arm for support. Or *amour*. Or both. "And who knows," he spluttered, "what might happen next."

Jill dialed a number on her cell phone and frowned. A shadow passed over her face. "He's not picking up."

"Who?" asked Myrtle.

"Cullen." Jill gave a martyred sigh. "He needs to stir the barbeque in the crock pot. Maybe he's fallen asleep. He's had a rough day today. I guess I'll have to go over and do it myself. Miles, it was great. I'll see you over at my place in a little while."

But before she could hurry away, Jill's sister, Willow floated up to the group in her flowing, hippy garb with an intense look on her pale face. She put out a hand and grasped Jill's arm in a tight grip. "Did you say you were going home?" Willow demanded. Myrtle was sure she'd heard Jill and was just determined to make a point.

Jill said shortly, "*Yes*, I'm going home. *No*, Cullen didn't pick up the phone. *Yes*, I've got to stir the meat and make sure everything is ready for guests. Anything else you wanted to ask?" She jutted out her chin.

For an allegedly peaceful person, Willow sure looked ready to pick a fight. "So where is he? If he's not *here* and he's not *there*, what's he doing? And why *isn't* he at home, helping you out? And I wonder where Sherry has gone. Have you noticed she's not at the party anymore?"

Jill's face flushed an unattractive purple.

"Did you know that everybody has been slipping over to your house tonight, bringing side dishes over? Know why? Because they know you can't afford to feed everybody. Now maybe if Cullen decided to find a job ... "

Jill gave a beneficent smile. "I'm well-aware of everyone's kindness. They're just being good friends, Willow. And working isn't Cullen's gift. And you know all about gifts, don't you? You're always talking about how the Creator endows each of us, animal and human, with particular gifts ... "

It was at this point that Willow made a sound that Myrtle thought at first had come from some kind of smoke detector or burglar alarm. "Cullen's talent is *drinking*, Jill. He doesn't even know how to *do* anything else."

Jill's cheery face turned into a mask of fury. She launched at Willow with a hissing sound and Myrtle watched in horror as the two started physically scrapping. The line for the bathroom was, however, determined to stay in place. Finally, it was Tiny Kirk, of all people, who came over to break up the scuffle. Jill yanked her arm away from Tiny, gave a huffy sigh, and headed right out the door. Willow looked suddenly deflated and unsure where she should go. She finally flitted off into Miles's living room where she lit on his sofa and looked blankly around her as if surprised to see a party in progress.

"You see," Myrtle said earnestly to Tippy Chambers in Miles's living room, "the problem with the supper club idea is that everyone's *spouses* come. So it's not just the dozen or so members, but their husbands, too. It *doubles* the number of people in a house."

"So what exactly are you saying, Myrtle? You think we need to limit the number of people who participate?"

Myrtle shook her head vigorously. "No, no. I'm saying I don't think this will work *at all*. I think we need to revert back to the book club. Back to a manageable number of people, back to meeting in the daytime. Back to books."

"But everyone was getting tired of the old book club, Myrtle. That's why we're doing something different."

Tippy really couldn't help the fact that she sounded so condescending, thought Myrtle. She'd just been wealthy for so long that the money was ingrained into her vocal chords.And *must* Tippy talk so loud? Myrtle wasn't deaf, but Tippy never seemed to remember that fact.

"Well of course I know that, Tippy. But I thought we could change the book club into a *real* book club. A new-and-improved version of the old one where we study the classics. No one would be bored with classic literature."

Tippy frowned at Myrtle like she wasn't sure she was following her. "The classics. Like *Valley of the Dolls*?"

Myrtle slumped. This would be harder than she'd realized. She looked up as Miles hurried past her, navigating through the crowd. The party seemed even more crowded into the small space. Had even *more* people come in? Were there party-crashers here? It seemed like the number had tripled and that the decibel level had tripled, too. Georgia Simpson was being especially loud. She'd somehow managed to get seriously drunk, even though supper club had started just half an hour before. Could she have *arrived* at the party drunk?

Georgia got even louder and coarser than usual. She hollered loudly at Simon Caulfield's wife, Libba, who was right in front of her and didn't need help with her hearing, "The flea market didn't have *squat*, lemme tell you. You'd think once in a while somebody'd cough up something decent from their closets and bring it in to sell. Nuthin'! There was nuthin' there. Not that I have any *money*. Not like *some* people."

Miles sidled up to Myrtle and murmured, "In the room the women come and go / Talking of Michelangelo."

Myrtle smiled. "Okay, Prufrock. Nice use of irony. She's toasted, obviously."

"Any more toasted," said Miles, "and we'd be scraping her over the kitchen sink with a knife."

Myrtle flinched as Erma Sherman came up and brayed, "This really is a treat. I don't get out at night much, you know. Not like Miss Myrtle Clover." She gave a haw-hawing laugh, making her sound even more like a donkey than she already did.

Myrtle froze at hearing her name and half-turned, eyeing Erma icily.

"Myrtle goes out every night for a two a.m. stroll, don't you?" Erma grinned crookedly. "I wonder sometimes if she's going out to visit a sweetheart."

"I don't go out *every* night," said Myrtle coldly. "And certainly not to see boyfriends when I do. I just have a little insomnia, that's all."

"A *little* insomnia?" Miles said under his breath. Myrtle was a raging insomniac. It was a wonder she functioned at all on the miniscule amount of sleep she did get.

"Besides," asked Myrtle, "what are *you* doing up at two a.m.?"

"I'm not *always* up. Just enough to notice when old ladies thump their canes down sidewalks."

Myrtle had no rejoinder to that, so just took a sip of her sherry and fumed. Fortunately, the focus changed to sleep problems in general with other people chiming in and the whole group walked off to get more wine.

"I *hate* living next door to her," Myrtle seethed to Miles. "I'm not that loud when I walk, am I?"

"Not that I've noticed. Of course, *I'm* usually up at two a.m., myself."

"Next time I walk by and see your lights on, I'll knock. We can scandalize Erma."

Georgia plucked up a napkin and put a handful of cheese straws on it, scattering them wildly as she did. Unaware of the mess she was making, she waved her hand. "Blanche!" she bellowed. "What'cha doing? I didn't think you'd be here, since you hate Jill an' all."

Myrtle moved in closer. Miles rolled his eyes at her nosiness and headed to the kitchen to bring in more wine.

Blanche started looking uneasily around her.

"You looking for her, too? When you find her, let me know. I'm planning to pop her right in the eye when I see her. Bam!" Georgia swayed forward and Blanche shrank away from her with a look of fascinated disgust. "Jill pulled a number on you, too, didn't she? I know allll about that, Blanche. Alllll about it."

At this somewhat cryptic statement, Blanche rushed off toward the back of the house, face blazing.

Georgia seemed to barely register that Blanche was gone as she stuffed the last remaining cheese straws—and part of the napkin—in her mouth. Myrtle wondered if it would be worth trying to ask Georgia anything while she was in this state. She might be able to strong-arm more information out of her while her guard was down, but the downside would be that Georgia's information might not make a whole lot of sense. She had a feeling that Georgia would be able to fill in the blanks regarding Blanche's hostility toward Jill.

Myrtle had just decided to give Georgia's cognitive skills a go when there was a sudden, piercing shriek. Erma Sherman waved her arms around in big circles, clearing people out of the way like a bulldozer. "My diamond earring!" she screeched. "It's gone! Everyone start looking!"

It was really amazing how quickly everyone followed Erma's orders. Fortunately, Myrtle had age on her side as an excellent excuse not to engage in the hunt. She looked as feeble as possible while doddering over to Miles's sofa. Everyone was on the floor, running their hands over the hardwood floors and area rugs. Erma wailed, "We've *got* to find it. It's worth a ton of money. *Real* diamonds. And a family heirloom ... "

At that moment, Miles pushed through the kitchen door with the tray full of red wine and tripped right over the back of Tippy Chambers. "Whooooaaaa!" The tray went flying and the drinks fell over the backs of the guests. There was glass and alcohol everywhere, Miles sprawled out over the floor, there was cussing from people who would need expensive dry cleaning, and plenty of general assorted chaos. Myrtle enjoyed the chaos from a distance.

"My diamond earring! Keep looking!" commanded Erma.

"I don't think anyone's going to risk being cut by broken glass right now," said Miles dryly as he carefully got up from the floor and adjusted his glasses on his nose. "Maybe while I'm cleaning up, I'll find it."

The party had definitely taken a turn for the worse. And unfortunately, Erma's lost earring looked like it might end up as the most newsworthy aspect of the evening. Sloan would be disappointed.

Many of the guests looked sweaty. Myrtle peered around the room. Too many people in a small space. Miles shoved open the windows as he passed them to let in more air. Simon Caulfield and his wife Libba walked past Myrtle. Simon continued stalking out the door, suit drenched, face furious.

Libba leaned over the sofa to speak to Myrtle. "Could you tell Miles thanks for us? Simon got covered with wine so we're heading home. Y'all have fun, though." She disappeared out the door behind her husband.

Miles stooped down by Myrtle a couple of minutes later to pick up part of a glass that had somehow managed to find its way across the room. "You've had some casualties. Simon and Libba have left the building."

Tippy walked up. "And Willow," she added with a sigh. "She got doused with wine and decided to change. I guess it doesn't matter if she's still changing when we get there as long as we can all get inside. Her house is next on the list."

"At this point," said Miles as he delicately held the shard of glass, "anyone who wants to evacuate is welcome to do so." He looked around him at the pandemonium. "Have you seen Sherry

Angevine anywhere? I was going to ask her something about her flower garden."

"Actually, no. I haven't seen her since early in the party. And I only really noticed her then because she had so much eye makeup on. She looks like one of those zombies from *Night of the Living Dead*," said Myrtle.

Tippy took the break from the earring search and smashed glass recovery to make an announcement. "Okay, everyone! For us to keep on track this evening, we need to move on to the next house. I'm sure Erma's earring hasn't walked out the door, so we'll leave Miles to look for it later tonight. Remember, we're going to Willow Pearce's house next for soups and salads, then to Jill's, before ending up at Myrtle's house for dessert. We're running a little bit behind," this with a reproving look at the careless Erma, who seemed completely unaware that she was being reproached, "so we'll probably spend just thirty minutes at Willow's."

They all tramped over to Willow's house, looking a bit like a well-sauced tour group with Tippy striding ahead as leader. Willow lived down the street from Miles in a smallish brick ranch on the non-lakefront side of the road. The road was lined with old sidewalks and shielded from the sun by ancient, massive trees on both sides. On Myrtle's side of the street, the houses backed up to the lake, and the other side, including Red's house, backed up to woods. The road curved to follow the line of the lake so Myrtle couldn't see the houses on the other side of the bend, including Willow's, Sherry's, and Jill's.

Willow hadn't left her front lights on, so Tippy called a group halt. "I'll go ahead and ask her to turn on the porch lights. I don't want our older ladies tripping."

Myrtle felt a little huffy about being classified as an "older lady," considering that Tippy was fairly old herself, just well-preserved. Tippy swept down the front walk, silks floating along behind her. A cat leapt out of a shadow, hissing, and Tippy gave a short shriek before a quick recovery. She rapped at the door, then cautiously opened it. Reaching inside, Tippy turned on the outdoor lights, revealing a tidy yard and an herb garden. "Willow?" called Tippy. She shrugged and motioned everyone to come in. "She *is* expecting us," she said.

It was clear when they walked in that Willow *had* been expecting them. She had bowls of covered tossed and pasta salads set out on the tables. Clearly, she was, at some level, anticipating their arrival. "Where is she?" asked Myrtle grumpily to Miles. "Really, this is carrying things too far. I know Willow is really New-Agey and everything, but not to be hostessing your own party is really too much. She could at least be asking us if we need tongs for the salad. Because, for heaven's sake, we need some tongs for the salad!"

Miles was about to answer her back when Willow finally drifted into the room, carrying yet another feline. She wore another flowing garment to replace the one that the wine had spilled on. Myrtle was sure that if she ventured into Willow's bedroom, that she would find an entire closet full of flowing, hippyesque garments. This one, at least, wasn't as bright as the one she'd been wearing at Miles's house.

Willow waved a vague hand. "Help yourselves, everyone."

The phone rang and Willow picked up a cordless receiver. "Oh hi Paul. Now? Where is the van? How many cats is it? No, that's fine, I'll be there in a few minutes." She hung up and glanced around for her car keys until finding them on a table. Willow put the cat down on the table and floated to the front door with her keys.

"Willow?" Tippy asked with a hard edge to her politely cultured voice. "You're not leaving your guests, are you?"

Willow said in a wispy voice, "Oh, yes, I need to. My friend trapped a whole colony of feral cats and was on his way to transport them to the clinic when his van broke down. I'll have to help him out. Myrtle knows all about it," she said. No Myrtle didn't, thought Myrtle. And Myrtle didn't want to.

Tippy looked nonplussed. "Right now? The cats have to be transported right *now*?" Myrtle had never heard such a shrill note in Tippy's voice before.

Willow tilted her head to one side. "The cats will be frightened, Tippy. They'll need to head over to the clinic for their spaying. Besides, the staff is waiting for them. And my friend is stranded, too."

Tippy opened her mouth again but Willow had already slipped out of the door.

"Well for heaven's sake," said Myrtle crossly. This supper club had been a perfectly rotten idea. If they'd been drinking a nice glass of chardonnay and talking about Dickens, this never would have happened.

Tippy clicked her tongue. "I'm not sure your supper club plan was such a wonderful idea, Myrtle." Several other members looked reproachfully at Myrtle.

"*My*—"

"Well, I guess there's nothing left to be done but assume responsibility for the hostess duties." Tippy immediately disappeared into the kitchen, and then returned with a pair of tongs. She manned the salad table and started helping plates. Myrtle scowled. She hadn't wanted to be here in the first place, Miles was still off cleaning up the mess at his house, and now she was feeling guilty about a party that hadn't been her idea to begin with. Then she sighed. Plus the fact she was supposed to be documenting the thing for Sloan's blog. She desolately pulled out her cell phone and snapped off a few pictures, unenthusiastically.

Maybe it was time for a small drink. She hadn't really imbibed at Miles's house since there was so much competition over the restroom facilities. She looked around her. No drinks. Not only were there no alcoholic beverages, there was no water, no iced tea, and no lemonade. She'd have to completely abandon her idea of drinking a glass of wine. Clearly, Willow's careful regard for her health extended to abstaining from alcohol. Darn her.

"Unforgiveable!" muttered Myrtle under her breath.

"There's no tea," murmured Tippy to Myrtle in a flat voice. Apparently, the dire lack of courtesy at Willow's house had put her in a state of shock.

"I'll see if there's any in the fridge that we can use. Surely Willow made some," said Myrtle.

"I can check," said Tippy quickly.

"Now Tippy, I'm not going to fall and break my neck in Willow's kitchen, I promise you." Tippy's overprotectiveness grated on Myrtle's nerves. She leaned on her cane and thumped off to Willow's kitchen.

It didn't look anything like Myrtle's own sunny, kitschy kitchen. Where Myrtle had red-checkered curtains, Willow had dark linen. Where Myrtle had natural light, Willow relied on lava lamps. And where Myrtle had candles for those rare candlelight suppers, Willow had incense. At least, thought Myrtle, Willow seemed to share Myrtle's affinity for roosters in the kitchen. At least on her potholders. Although roosters didn't seem to jive with the otherworldly theme of the décor, Myrtle thought as she rummaged through Willow's refrigerator, which was stuffed with organic foods. Myrtle finally found, behind the tofu, cut up vegetables in zipper bags, and heads of broccoli and cabbage, a pitcher of iced tea shoved way in the back.

Everyone heaped their plates. At least the food looked decent, even if Willow had flaked out. Actually, thought Myrtle, all in all there seemed to be an overwhelming amount of drama going on. Blanche looked like she'd been run over by a truck, which was probably the strain of being around Jill. Even though she hadn't noticed Jill in a while. Not since she left Miles's house to go stir the barbeque. But Blanche could still be stressed out, just worried they were going to have a run in. Myrtle couldn't imagine Jill starting something with Blanche at a supper club, though she *had* gotten into a fight with her own sister there.

Sherry had surfaced from wherever she'd been. She seemed to have even more eye makeup on and looked like the cat that'd eaten the canary. She was rumpled, keyed up, and laughing very loudly at something Blanche was saying. And Myrtle was pretty sure that Blanche was in no mood to be funny.

Miles was back, face flushed from his cleaning exertions. But he looked unhappy about being there.

Erma Sherman was in an uncharacteristically hushed mood and kept fingering the earlobe where the missing diamond earring used to reside. Myrtle was just relieved to have a break from Erma's usual foolishness.

Much of the salad seemed to be falling onto the floor. The intoxication of many of Willow's guests was likely to blame. Miles walked up to Myrtle and said, "I'm going to run back home for a few minutes. Just in case anyone is looking for me."

"Must be your Type-A nature kicking in. Are you fretting over the red wine stains on your carpet?"

Miles shrugged a shoulder. "Just a little. Most of it fell on hardwoods, but I did pay a lot for those throw rugs. I'll just run over there and press on the stains with some paper towels. I'll be back before we go over to Jill's house for the barbeque."

Plenty of women noticed that Miles had left. The older, female population of Bradley paid close attention whenever there was a new, eligible, attractive, older man in town. They brought over their tastiest casseroles, being sure to say that it was so *hard* cooking for one person—could he please take the extra helpings? They dressed up in their prettiest dresses for book club and wore carefully-applied makeup. And Miles was still considered a newcomer. The way Bradley operated, he'd probably *still* be considered a newcomer ten years from now. His obituary would probably read "Miles Standish, a recent resident of Bradley, died …."

Erma grabbed Myrtle's arm tightly. "Where is Miles, Myrtle? Where did he go?"

Myrtle shook her arm free in irritation. "He's gone home to clean up the mess, Erma. He didn't want the stains to set and he didn't spend much time on stain removal before he came to Willow's."

"I've got to catch up with him," said Erma breathlessly. "What if he forgets about my earring? He might throw it away with the trash!" She barreled out of the house.

Willow's portion of the progressive dinner wasn't nearly as lively as Miles's. Time seemed to drag on and on. There was an audible sigh of relief from the group when Tippy announced it was time to head over to Jill's house.

The guests were more muted this time as they walked. Myrtle felt worn out from the evening and everyone else was probably the same. In contrast to Willow's house, Jill's house was brightly lit both outside and inside. Tippy breathed a sigh of relief. "I'm glad we're going to Jill's," she said. "I don't like playing hostess at someone else's house. And Jill is always so on top of things."

"Jill will be more organized than her sister," agreed Myrtle.

But Jill *wasn't* on top of things enough to greet the party at the door, which was a bit of a surprise. Tippy cautiously opened the front door and peeped in. "Jill?" she asked. She hesitated. "Maybe she just had to run in the back for a minute. She *is* expecting us!" Tippy gave a forced laugh as the scenario at Willow's house repeated itself.

The group walked quietly through the front door. Miles caught up with them from behind and gave Myrtle a questioning look. "Jill's AWOL," she said quietly.

"Jill?" called Tippy again. She wavered before calling, "Cullen?" Sherry, their next-door-neighbor, seemed to think that Cullen might need a louder summons. "*Cullen!*" she hollered.

Cullen walked in, looking hung-over. Or maybe still drunk, Myrtle wasn't sure. He registered the large group of people at his door. "Oh, the supper club," he said. Then, "Where's Jill?"

"You tell us!" retorted Myrtle. What was wrong with this family? Had they never thrown a party before?

"Maybe she's in the kitchen. She could have plugged in her headphones and not be able to hear us."

"When she's expecting company at any minute?" asked Tippy dubiously. Even Tippy's ladylike manner was slipping after all the rudeness she'd observed over the evening.

"This," said Myrtle in an aside to Tippy, "is exactly why we should give up on a supper club and return to the book club model. This would *never* happen if we were all eating cucumber sandwiches, drinking iced tea, and reading *Pride and Prejudice*."

They opened the kitchen door and stopped short. They'd found Jill, all right. Lying on the floor with a puddle of blood under her head and a cast iron skillet lying next to her.

Chapter Four

The next few minutes were complete pandemonium. There was shrieking, people bumping into each other, and several simultaneous calls to the police. Cullen looked like he'd been punched in the stomach. Sherry competently poured him a drink and pushed it into his hand, although Myrtle was fairly sure that Cullen didn't need anything else to drink that night.

"I think," Miles's voice rose through the cacophony, "that everyone needs to step outside. Probably all the way to the sidewalk, so the police can pull up in the driveway. We're probably trampling on potential evidence."

Everyone poured out the door, some more eagerly than others. "I knew," mused Myrtle aloud to Miles, "that supper club would mean disaster."

"It's been nothing but disaster tonight," agreed Miles. "And it's too bad about Jill."

Myrtle nodded gloomily. "I know, it's terrible. I liked her. Despite the rummaging around in the medicine cabinet thing." She saw the lights of a police car approaching and felt suddenly very sad. "Such a shame."

Red's car pulled into Jill and Cullen's driveway and Red stepped out, still buttoning up parts of his uniform. He strode over to his mother. "It's you—the professional body locator. Where is she?"

"The kitchen," she said.

Red gave everyone instructions to stay back away from the house and grounds and walked in the front door, dialing on his cell phone as he went.

"Probably calling in the state police," said Myrtle. "They'll need to have a forensic team here. And I suppose he's going to have to question us." She paused. "You know, Miles, we're probably one of the last ones to see her alive. She was calling Cullen when she suddenly left to go home. Right after her big fight with Willow."

The police questioning wasn't nearly as interesting as Myrtle had hoped. The state police let many people go home, and the statement she gave was fairly brief, as was everyone's, probably. There hadn't been much to report, after all—Jill had been at Miles's house, talked to a few of the guests, waited for the restroom, made a phone call, fought with Willow, and gone home to check on the food. When the supper club had arrived at Jill's house, she was already dead. Myrtle did notice that Red and his deputy were trying to get an idea where everyone was when the party was taking place.

Myrtle remembered lots of coming and going during the party. Red and the state police were going to have their hands full.

Miles waited for Myrtle to finish her statement before walking home with her. Red gave Miles an appreciative wave when he saw them set out. "I guess Red wanted you to deliver me safely back home?"

"Well, there *is* a murderer running around, you know."

"I doubt they'd want to kill *me*, though. Not yet, anyway."

Miles gave her a hard look. "You're not putting on your detective hat again, are you? Last time you almost got yourself killed."

"There are several very good reasons why I want to get involved, Miles. For one, I did like Jill and I'm sorry she's dead. For another—it delights my very soul when I solve mysteries before Red does. Plus, of course, I'm a newspaper reporter. I'm just following the story."

"You really just write a helpful hints column, Myrtle. You aren't a reporter covering a beat, you know."

"That's where you're wrong, Miles. Sloan has me writing extra news stories for the new *Bradley Bugle* blog. Which makes another excellent reason for my getting involved. Let's just say that I *am* covering the story. What could you add to it? Did you see or hear anything unusual?"

Miles nodded, slowly. "Well, there's something unusual at my house right now, actually."

"What?"

"Georgia. Passed out in the back bedroom."

"Miles! What will you do with her?"

"I won't have my wicked way with her, Myrtle, if that's what you're implying. I *was* planning on getting Red to help me heave her back home but that plan has changed now that Red's evening is looking like a busy one."

"How long has she been back there?" Myrtle tried in vain to remember the last time she saw Georgia. She seemed to remember taking a picture of her at some point when she was acting particularly obnoxious at Miles's house.

"I was trying to figure that out," said Miles, pushing his glasses up his nose. "I don't think I remember seeing her after she'd upset Blanche at my house."

"I guess that takes her off the suspects list for Jill's murder," said Myrtle. "'She'd have been a prime candidate, too ... what with her Jill hatred and all."

Miles shook his head. "I don't think it gives her an alibi at all. She could easily have stumbled out my back door and headed over to Jill's house. Several people warned me tonight that Georgia can have a horrible temper when she's drunk ... .they told me to keep my eye on her. So she could have gone over there to have it out with Jill, clobbered her on the head with the skillet, and then staggered back over to my house to fall asleep."

"Wouldn't she be covered with blood?" asked Myrtle with a small shiver.

"Not necessarily. There might have been a little spattering, but on the whole, probably not too much."

"Do you want *me* to try to help you with Georgia?" asked Myrtle. Could Georgia possibly make any sense at this part of the evening? Maybe it would be the best time to talk to her—if she started spilling secrets.

"I don't think that's a good idea," said Miles as they passed his house on the way to Myrtle's. "You'd be off-balance with your cane and everything. Maybe Elaine could help me. Do you think she's still up? You could stay in Red and Elaine's house with Jack while Elaine is gone." He added in a persuasive voice as Myrtle set her lip, "You won't get any sense out of Georgia tonight. She was talking nonsense the first time I tried to wake her up. That's when I decided just to let her sleep."

Myrtle shrugged. She sat in the house and watched out the window as Elaine and Miles helped a staggering Georgia back to her house.

Under ordinary circumstances, Myrtle would have been happily gossiping with suspects and eking out information the day after a murder.

Unhappily, however, she was instead on her way to volunteer at the Kiwanis Club's pancake breakfast. She couldn't let the Kiwanis Club down—Red, though, would end up paying some consequences soon.

"Myrtle," teased Miles with a smile, as stood next to her in the buffet line, "Volunteering out of the goodness of her heart."

Myrtle scowled and waved a spatula threateningly at him.

"And volunteering the morning after a murder—that's real dedication."

Myrtle now attempted to pretend he wasn't next to her in the serving line. How did she get the job of serving pancakes when an actual Kiwanis member merely had the job of pointing out there was both apple and orange juice?

"Remind me again why Red set you up with this gig? What meddling were you doing that made him decide to find busywork for you?"

Myrtle narrowed her eyes, "I didn't meddle one bit. Red's behaving extremely irrationally. In fact, I worry about the welfare and safety of Bradley citizens with Red at the helm. Red takes his law and his order just a little too seriously."

They heard a booming belly-laugh close by. Miles jumped. "That laugh ... " He frowned as he tried to remember.

"Georgia Simpson."

"Ahh, right. The sweet magnolia blossom of the South. Who passes out drunk in strangers' houses?"

"Better watch it, Miles. Don't think she won't knock you into next week. She won't make any allowances for the fact you're volunteering at the Kiwanis pancake breakfast." Then Myrtle smiled sweetly at Georgia as she approached. "One pancake or two?"

"Two of the biggest you've got, Miss Myrtle. None of those dainty baby ones, okay? I've got to get fortified for my day today." She thumped at her stomach.

Georgia clearly wanted to be asked about her day and Miles appeared to be at a total loss for words. "So what's on your agenda today?" asked Myrtle, obediently, as she put two of the heftier pancakes on her plate. "Some exciting judo on the schedule?" Miles gave a helpless groan next to her as if he feared her imminent demise. "I'm not being facetious. Miles, you might not know this, but Georgia is a black belt in judo."

Georgia grinned. "And the best in the state of North Carolina, according to my last tournament. But no, I'm trolling for angels today." To Miles, who was still trying to digest this statement, she bellowed, "Milk, OJ, and apple juice? Where the hell's the coffee?"

"Not my jurisdiction," said Miles, waving a hand across the room to a table set up with all the coffee fixings.

"Trolling for angels," said Myrtle thoughtfully as she stuck a pancake on someone else's plate. "That's right, you and Jill Caulfield used to visit yard sales on Saturday mornings, didn't you? You collect angel figurines, right? I remember you were even doing that in high school."

Georgia's face became a mask of hostility. Myrtle frowned. Was it the mention of angels? High school? Or had accidentally served Georgia dainty pancakes?

"Jill," spat Georgia, "was no friend of *mine,* Miss Myrtle. That cow robbed people of their money. Robbed them! I'm not sorry she's gone. And you shouldn't be, either."

"We'll be sure to take that under advisement," said Miles hurriedly.

Myrtle wasn't done yet. "But I am, Georgia. Jill was my employee—she did some cleaning for me." She absently put two more pancakes on someone else's plate and Miles vaguely gestured to the juice.

Georgia leaned in as close to Myrtle as she could with the serving table between them. "Well obviously she musta not found anything she could use against you in the days she cleaned for you. Thank your lucky stars that she's dead. Whups— pancakes getting cold." And with that, she plodded off to a table.

Elaine and Jack were two of the last customers in the line. Elaine had Jack on one hip, which she kept turned away from the serving line while she gestured to the bacon, sausage, eggs and pancakes and pushed along two plates. Myrtle took one of the plates and heaped it full of food and carried it to a table before doing the same with another plate. "Miles, my time is up. Can you handle it from here?" She was pleased that there wasn't the slightest bit of sarcasm in her voice. It wasn't like Miles's juice duty was such a heavy load to bear.

"I didn't know you were going to be here today, Elaine." She scooted her chair over and Elaine plopped Jack into a high chair and sat down next to Myrtle.

"I thought I needed to offer you a little moral support, considering Red was the one who got you into this." She cut into her pancakes, putting some on Jack's tray. His small hand closed into a fist over the food, stuffing it into his mouth. "How did your shift go?" she asked.

"It was okay. But don't tell Red that. Next thing I know he'll have me doing a worthy cause a week."

"Mm. I saw the gnomes were still out there this morning."

"*Precious,* aren't they? Red can enjoy the scenery for a while," Myrtle scrubbed at some butter that had found its way into Jack's wispy red hair. "I did hear something interesting when I was in the serving line."

Jack had bored with eating the pancakes by this time and now busily rubbed them into his hair. Maybe he thought that's what Myrtle had been doing. Fortunately, Elaine was preoccupied with sugaring and creaming her coffee or else the entire rest of the breakfast would be consumed by Elaine scrubbing at Jack's head. "What was that?" asked Elaine.

"Georgia Simpson was downright furious with Jill Caulfield."

"What? I thought they were BFFs."

It drove Myrtle nuts when Elaine used texting language in conversations. At her age, too! "I'd thought they were going to be Best Friends Forever, too," said Myrtle, pointedly drawing out the acronym. "But money apparently came between them."

Elaine furrowed her brows. "Money? How is that possible ... .they're not related or anything. How does money come between friends?"

"Maybe Jill wouldn't lend Georgia money? Or maybe Jill wouldn't pay Georgia back on a loan she made? I'm not sure. But

I thought it was interesting that Saint Jill had more enemies than any of us realized."

"Surely Georgia isn't an *enemy*. But it's too bad they weren't friends any more. I thought everybody liked Jill." Then Elaine snapped her fingers. "I almost forgot!" She pulled up a big canvas tote bag from the floor and rifled through it, removing zipper bags of cereal, baby wipes, and disposable bibs. "Here it is." She pulled out a plastic bag full of cat food and several printouts and put them on the table next to Myrtle.

Myrtle looked at Elaine with concern. It was clear the stress of mommyhood and Elaine's constant search for new, intellectually stimulating avenues to pursue had started affecting her brain. Elaine loved Jack dearly, but wasn't finding her sole calling in diaper changing, cleaning up spilled Cheerios, and chopping carrots into bite-sized snacks. With every new project Elaine took on, Myrtle saw her get more and more scatter-brained.

"Cat food. Very nice, Elaine. Sorry ... what's this for, again?"

"Friends of Ferals," she said eagerly.

"Feral whats?" asked Myrtle with some trepidation.

"Cats," said Elaine. "Oh, don't look like that. It's not what you think."

"I think you're going to end up like one of those kooky ladies with fifty cats draped over their kitchen appliances. Like Willow. Remember how nutty she was last night? Think of Jack, Elaine! Where will he find room to toddle around?"

"It's not like that at all, Myrtle. The idea is that you reduce the feral cat population by capturing the cats, taking them to a vet to get fixed, then releasing them again to the wild. They don't come inside. They shouldn't! It wouldn't fit their lifestyle. Besides, you're the whole reason I've gotten interested in Friends of Ferals."

Myrtle wasn't so sure she wanted to be held up as the inspiration for such a membership. "Why? Oh—you mean because of that stray that's been lurking around my backyard. I'm not sure it needs a friend. It seems to be doing quite well on its own by decimating the population at my birdfeeder."

"Just take a look at this information when you have a chance. After all," Elaine noted archly, "elderly detectives and cats seem to go together."

Elaine glanced Jack's way and froze. His red hair stuck up in little yellow spikes all over his head and he was now rubbing buttery pancakes onto his shirt. "Jack!"

So much for that conversation, thought Myrtle, sipping her orange juice.

"Mind if I take a seat?" asked a deep voice behind Myrtle. She stiffened as Red sat down next to her with a heaping plate of pancakes. A puckish look of mischief made him appear younger than his forty-five years. If you ignored the fact that gray was quickly invading the red hairs that had given him his nickname, he could pass for a much younger man.

"How did your volunteer work go this morning?" asked Red innocently. Myrtle fired him a look that should have curdled milk. "It was annoying timing, Red. I would rather have been home, grieving Jill."

"Grieving *Jill*?" Red's voice was incredulous. "Why on earth would you be doing that?"

"I'd gotten really fond of her," said Myrtle with a sniff. "She livened Bradley up a little bit."

"With her stellar housekeeping?"

"With her personality. She has her enemies, you know. She stirred things up." Myrtle looked at him sideways, waiting for him to register that she was a fount of information. Red seemed more interested in playing peek-a-boo with a chuckling Jack. "*One* of her enemies is sitting in this very room," intoned Myrtle in an ominous voice.

Finally she'd gotten Red's attention. "Who might that be?"

"Georgia. "

"And why exactly," asked Red, studying the tattooed Georgia who was innocently shoveling pancakes down her throat, "would Georgia be Jill's enemy?"

"That's for me to know and you to find out," said Myrtle smugly. Let Elaine fill him in later, if she wanted to. Myrtle certainly wouldn't.

Red growled and Elaine quickly interrupted. "Red, how is the investigation going? He was at the Caulfield's house the rest of the night," Elaine told Myrtle. "He never did come home."

This reminder served to make Red look even more exhausted. He rubbed his eyes. Myrtle opened her mouth to remind him how bad rubbing was for eyes, but snapped it shut again. She didn't want to interrupt him right when he was about to talk about the case. "Just a lot going on. Of course we had Lieutenant Perkins and his crew from the state police and forensics there. Cullen Caulfield was acting like an idiot, which didn't help. He didn't want us messing around in his house. And then some of your charming supper club members," here he rolled his eyes at Myrtle, "wanted their Pyrex dishes back. And Erma Sherman wouldn't go away and kept saying it 'was such a shame about all that barbeque going to waste' and wouldn't we just put a cooler of it outside and everyone could have some before it went bad?" Red frowned at the memory.

"Well the supper club's obsession with casserole dishes and plasticware doesn't shock me at all. But what exactly does 'acting like an idiot' entail?"

"Cullen was just basically underfoot. He didn't want to leave the house and he wanted to hover right beside us at all times. I swear he was either still drunk or had a flask on him and was continuing to drink. Then, when we started questioning him, he fell apart. Cried, ranted. The whole nine yards."

Myrtle leaned forward. "You questioned him?"

"Well, naturally. Whenever a married person is a homicide victim, the spouse is automatically a prime suspect. That's just Police Investigation 101."

"Was he crying because he was upset about Jill? Or was he upset for some other reason?" asked Myrtle.

"I think he was worried about his own hide, mostly. And then he was just mad that he was a suspect at all. Said he was 'grieving.' And that he had a gun and by-golly, if he was going to kill Jill, he'd of shot her. What kind of man would kill his wife with a skillet? he asked." Red rubbed his eyes again.

"Don't rub your eyes," said Myrtle absently. "It's not good for them." She pondered a moment. "Why *wouldn't* he have killed her with his gun? And why on earth would he have chosen the supper club night to murder his wife? It's not like he didn't have ample opportunity on days when no one was visiting."

"Who knows? Maybe they had a big argument and it was a heat of the moment kind of thing." Red's eyes narrowed. "You sound entirely too interested in these proceedings, Mama."

"Just like everyone else, Red. Don't worry, I won't invade your territory," said Myrtle caustically. "So what *did* you do?"

"With what?"

"With all that barbeque? And the Tupperware?"

"Well, the forensic guys were basically done with the kitchen this morning. So I set everyone's dishes outside in the garage so they could pick them up. I was getting three or four phone calls an hour from those women, so I was ready to get them off my back."

"That's funny," said Myrtle. "No one called me up to ask about the uneaten desserts at my house. We didn't even make it to the dessert portion of the evening. You'd think they'd be asking about all the desserts I had planned for the group."

Red wisely said nothing, but rolled his eyes at Elaine. Myrtle saw the look and pressed her lips together in irritation. Her cooking wasn't *that* bad. How horrible did everyone think it was that they'd pass on free sweets?

"And the ill-fated barbeque?" asked Myrtle, changing the subject.

"Not ill-fated at all. Jill had kept the barbeque warm in a couple of slow cookers. It might have gotten a little dried-out, but it was still good. Cullen didn't want it, so I stuck it outside in the garage, too. Erma Sherman thoughtfully provided a large cooler," added Red sarcastically.

Myrtle thought about this. "Was there a lot of barbeque?"

"Well, sure. Enough to feed thirty people, I guess."

Myrtle stood up. "I'm thinking about running by and getting myself a little supper. Seeing as how it was going to waste and everything."

"It's good of you to worry about wasted food, Mama." Red eyed her suspiciously.

"Don't forget your cat food!" Elaine picked up the baggie and handed it to her before she was successfully able to escape.

Chapter Five

Getting barbeque was as good an excuse as any to go over to Jill's house and snoop around outside a bit, thought Myrtle. Bradley was one of those towns where there was bound to be some people standing around the Caulfields' house, talking. And Myrtle wouldn't mind listening to them.

Jill's house looked quiet and there were no rubberneckers as far as Myrtle could see. The rush for barbeque and Tupperware must have died down. Myrtle walked into the garage and saw Erma's huge cooler there and a perky looking sign in Erma's schoolgirl scrawl that said: "Free Barbeque. Help Yourself!" It had a smiley face on it. It was a sign that refused to acknowledge that a violent death had occurred mere yards away.

Myrtle also saw Willow there. And Willow looked taken aback when she saw her. "Willow," said Myrtle, leaning on her cane, "I am so sorry about poor Jill. I just feel sick about it."

Willow looked pretty sick herself. She was even paler than usual and her white hair hung lankly down. She didn't look like she'd showered and Myrtle wondered if the clothes she was wearing were the same ones she'd slept in. Willow swayed on her feet and Myrtle wondered if she were going to faint ... or throw up. Myrtle hesitated between recoiling and moving forward.

"Did you leave some Tupperware here?" asked Myrtle. "Red mentioned something about leaving the dishes outside."

"I didn't make it over here last night, remember? I had to go help Paul with the cats."

"Here," said Myrtle, feeling alarmed. "You're looking very sick, Willow." She ushered her over to a short brick wall that edged the garage and sat her down. "Sit here for a minute."

She watched Willow's pale face and red eyes and said, "Are you here to visit Cullen then? Since you don't have any dishes to pick up?"

Anger flashed briefly in Willow's eyes. Did she think Cullen was the killer? "No," she said fiercely, "I wasn't here to visit Cullen. I ... " she gestured over to the cooler. "I came for some of the barbeque. So we wouldn't waste it. Erma called me early this morning. I brought a plastic container with me." Willow held up a Tupperware container with her name written on the side.

Myrtle pressed her lips together in a grim line. She bet Erma *did* call Willow this morning. Maybe it was under the *guise* of leftovers, but it was pure nosiness that would have driven her.

"I'm sure there'll be women from the church running by with some casseroles for you, you know. There's a whole army that jumps into action after a death." Myrtle hesitated, then decided to ask, "What on earth do you think happened in there, Willow? Who'd have murdered Jill?"

Willow gave a strangled sob and Myrtle awkwardly patted her arm. "I'm so sorry, Willow. Never mind, if you don't want to talk about it. Such a shock," she murmured.

Willow collected herself. "Did you come over for some food, too?"

Myrtle had the grace to blush. At least she had the excuse of the container. Although it was one of those disposable kinds and she'd never intended on getting it back in the first place.

Fortunately, Willow got distracted by the bags Myrtle was still clutching. "Is that ... cat food?" asked Willow with more interest than she'd shown in the rest of the conversation.

Myrtle stopped herself just in time from making a face and instead put on what she hoped was a Saint Myrtle of Stray Kitties expression. "Well, yes. Yes it is. I have a feral feline friend in my backyard that's decided to adopt me. And I want to take care of my little furry buddy."

Willow beamed. "Friends of Ferals is a wonderful group. Elaine recently joined, didn't she? Our animal friends *need* us, you know. I just let Kojak—he's Cullen and Jill's dog," her voice faltered over Jill's name, "off that chain in the backyard. He needed rescuing. That poor animal," she said passionately. "I'd bring him back home with me but Cullen would demand him back. He doesn't care about Kojak a bit—he doesn't want him happy. And the poor dog would be happy with me." Animals seemed to be the one topic that made Willow animated. Besides complaining about Cullen, that is.

Myrtle was quickly losing interest in the conversation. Willow's brain had shifted gears now and Myrtle doubted there was any way to switch it back. "Yes. Well, I should be getting home to put the cat food out."

"And a bowl full of water," Willow called after her as Myrtle hustled away. She turned back to say good-bye to Willow and caught sight of Sherry Angevine peeking out behind one of Cullen's curtains.

Myrtle didn't really feel like going back home yet. She felt more like mulling things over with Miles. On the way back home, she stopped by Miles's house. A minute went by. Myrtle frowned and looked in Miles's driveway again. His car was there. She guessed he *could* have walked into town, but Miles usually drove since he'd been so accustomed to living in the city. She rang the doorbell.

Another minute passed before Miles's face peered out of the window next to his front door. Myrtle swore she saw irritation flash across his face. He slowly opened the door.

Myrtle gaped at him. "Miles! You're in your bathrobe and slippers!"

"That's not a crime, is it, Myrtle?" asked Miles with dignity.

"But it's the middle of the day!"

Miles shook his head in exasperation. "For heaven's sake, Myrtle. I simply decided to go back to bed after I left Kiwanis. I haven't been sleeping well lately, to begin with. Then last night we discovered a murder, I had to drag Georgia out of my house, I woke up at the crack of dawn to serve pancakes this morning—it's all made me completely exhausted. I'm a little better now that I've slept for—oh, only about forty-five minutes. Thanks for your concern."

His annoyance had a subduing effect on Myrtle. "Do you need coffee?" she asked meekly. "I could make some for us."

Myrtle made a pot of coffee while Miles changed into some jeans and a button down shirt. He eased himself onto his leather sofa and said, 'So give me an update. How are things going with the investigation this morning? Solved the case yet?"

Myrtle carefully ignored the trace of sarcasm in his voice. "No, it wasn't all that interesting this morning. Red didn't have much information to give me about the case, not that that's anything new. Or if he *had* information, he wasn't sharing any of it. Except he mentioned that Cullen was acting unusually."

"Unusually for Cullen or unusual for a regular person?"

"I guess for either one. The spouse is always suspect number one, you know, so I guess he was angry that the police were treating him as if he might have killed Jill. Then I saw Willow and she looked terrible ... "

"Well, her sister was murdered," said Miles.

" ... .but she says she came back to Jill's house for some of the leftover barbeque from last night. But I *think* she was actually there to confront Cullen and was just using the barbeque for an excuse. I bet she's pegged Cullen for the murderer."

"That would make sense," agreed Miles, "since she's never liked Cullen."

They sipped their coffee for a few minutes in silence.

"Did I tell you about my new friend?" asked Myrtle.

"You mean the furry, wild friend? Yes, you mentioned it. How are things going with it?"

"I think things are about to get even better." She held up the zippered bag with the cat food. "Elaine gave me some food for her. Although really, she eats like a king. You know how Erma's squirrel population always spills over into my yard? Wiping out the sunflower seeds in my feeder?"

Miles nodded.

"Well now the squirrels are terrified to even tiptoe into my yard. That cat is so fast that the squirrels never know what hit them."

"So this ferocious animal is female?" asked Miles. He pursed his lips doubtfully. "Are you sure about that?"

"Quite sure. It's female and tough as nails. Elaine wasn't kidding when she said these cats aren't adoptable. It's quite antisocial and temperamental," said Myrtle with satisfaction.

"Isn't it interesting," drawled Miles, "how animals can have so much in common with their owners?"

Miles ramblings were going to bore her again ... if she paid attention. Which she had no intention of doing. "I know you were taking a nap and everything, but what do you think about investigating with me?"

Miles's face left no doubt what he thought of that idea. "Really, Myrtle ... "

"I know. You'd rather be reading Faulkner. But I could use the help." She leaned heavily on her cane to remind him of her age and infirmity.

He sighed. "Help with what?"

"I'm going to try to catch up with Sherry in a little while. I saw her inside Cullen's house when I was leaving it today." Myrtle wiggled her eyebrows at Miles.

"That's not so strange, is it? After all, *you* were over at Cullen's house. And it sounds like Willow was there. Actually, it sounds like half the book club was over getting barbeque."

"Absolutely. We were all *at* Cullen's house. Not *in* Cullen's house. That's a big difference in prepositions. Anyway, I think it might be a good idea to touch base with Sherry and see what's up. You can set a clock by her weekend schedule—she always goes out to garden at two o'clock on Saturdays. She lives right next door to the Caulfields, so maybe she heard or saw something. Or has an idea who might have done it. Maybe she's having some sort of relationship with Cullen."

"Or maybe," said Miles in a dry voice, "she was just being a good neighbor and trying to see if Cullen needed any help this morning."

"You're illustrating my point exactly. We don't *know* why she was there this morning. But we'll find out. Because," Myrtle drew herself up stiffly, "Jill's death must be avenged. Justice must prevail!"

"Help with *what*? You still haven't told me what you need help with."

"Oh." Myrtle thought hard. Really, she just wanted a sidekick with her. It was practically a detective prerequisite. But she wasn't sure Miles was totally sold on the sidekick idea. "Listening to Sherry. She's a soft-talker, you know. It's hard for my old ears to catch everything she says."

Miles frowned, "I haven't noticed that Sherry is a—"

"So," said Myrtle hurriedly, "if you could just meet me outside Sherry's house at two o'clock. That'll give us a little time to eat some lunch and put our feet up for a few minutes. Okay! See you then."

Myrtle bustled out, leaving Miles to wonder how his day had gotten hijacked so quickly.

Myrtle fixed herself a sandwich and some chips for lunch and watched soap operas for a few minutes with her feet up. Completely refreshed, she decided to jump right into her investigation. Myrtle looked wistfully around her living room. Dust was already starting to collect. She missed energetic, cheerful, cleaning sensation Jill. She could easily have put up with the nosiness—there wasn't anything in her medicine cabinet that was interesting, anyway. The conversation, company, and cleaning would have made up for any privacy loss.

Sure enough, Sherry was outside promptly at two wearing ratty gardening gloves and a wide-brimmed, flowered hat. She bent down to pull some intrepid weeds that sprouted by her mailbox, then noticed Myrtle standing there. "Hi, Miss Myrtle. Getting some exercise?"

Sherry was always one to get right to the point, so Myrtle decided not to tiptoe around the issue. "I am. I always find that a little exercise helps with stress. And, with poor Jill's murder ... " Myrtle shrugged helplessly.

A cloud passed over Sherry's face. Literally. So Myrtle couldn't read her expression as well as she would have liked. "I know. It was *awful.*" Sherry paused. "But there's something even worse."

"Worse than the murder? But ... "

"Oh, here comes Miles. He's a nice guy, isn't he?"

About time, thought Myrtle. Some sidekick.

"Wait ... .I guess he's going back inside," said Sherry.

"Must have forgotten something," said Myrtle in a cross voice.

"Oh Lord. Heads-up, it's Erma Sherman."

"Helloooooo!" called out Erma in her nasal voice. "You're not *exercising*, are you, Myrtle? I mean, I know you walk to get places because you're too old to drive, but I didn't know you walked for fun, too!"

Myrtle frowned discouragingly at Erma. "Exercise is supposed to be good for me. Besides ... "

"I'm sure it is, Myrtle. Maybe you'll even live to be ninety!" said Erma kindly. "I walk every day!" She stood her stocky body tall and upright, at attention. Then she relaxed and laughed. "Glad I saw you out here, Myrtle. I wanted to let you know that I saw something at the hardware store yesterday that should help you with your crabgrass epidemic. Maybe you'll want to check it out. Just take your walk tomorrow in that direction. Crabgrass can take over everything, you see." She looked sagely at Myrtle through her thick glasses.

"Thanks for the advice," Myrtle said tartly. "But as I told you before, it's really *your* yard that's ... "

"Well, got to get going. Can't afford to let my heart rate slow down, you know. Toodle-oo!" Myrtle watched with great relief as she charged back off.

"Does she *have* a heart rate?" asked Sherry. "She's like Frankenstein. I don't know how you stand living next door to her." Sherry paused. "Almost as bad as living next to Jill."

Myrtle leaned in on her cane. "What do you mean?"

"That's what I was talking about before Erma bulldozed her way into our conversation." Sherry lowered her voice to a pitch that Myrtle had trouble hearing. "What's worse than the murder is that I'm *glad* she's dead."

Myrtle nodded attentively and Sherry continued. "To be perfectly honest, Miss Myrtle, Jill Caulfield drove me nuts for *years*. Talk about keeping up with the Joneses. There was no way in hell you could keep up with Jill. She'd be out here with her scissors, trimming some tiny shaggy spot near her curb. You never noticed when her flowers faded because she'd replace them with others. And *don't* get me started on her Christmas decorations!" Sherry was red in the face by this time.

Myrtle thought a moment. "I think I remember cars driving by just to look at the decorations." At Sherry's nod, Myrtle said, "A huge line of cars, actually."

"The Jill Caulfield Christmas Spectacular started in November and didn't stop until January. My bedroom was lit up like it was daytime."

Myrtle mulled through this information. "Maybe Jill spent so much time in her yard because she was trying to get away from Cullen. Do you think they had a happy marriage?"

This was apparently a bad subject, as Sherry's face seemed to shut down. Belatedly, Myrtle remembered that Sherry had had a terrible marriage, a horrible divorce proceeding, and had vowed never to marry again. Myrtle changed the subject before Sherry decided that her weeding really did need to be underway.

"Anyway, who do you think could have done it? I thought everyone really liked Jill," Myrtle said in a gossipy voice.

Sherry relaxed a little. "I think most people did. And, just because I didn't, it doesn't mean that I *killed* her, of course," she stressed.

"Since you're next door, did you see or hear anything last night that might give us a clue to what happened?" Myrtle did her best to conjure up a gossipy old lady voice.

"But I wasn't at home to hear or see anything, Miss Myrtle. Remember? I was at the progressive dinner with you. Remember how we talked there?" Sherry studied Myrtle with concern, as if sure Myrtle was losing it.

Myrtle frowned. She remembered talking to Sherry at Miles's house. But she was sure that there was a period of time when Sherry hadn't been around. "Of course I remember talking to you. Am I your alibi for the evening? Do you think you need one?"

Sherry shrugged. "It was common knowledge that Jill drove me nuts as a neighbor. And I've heard Red and that other cop want to talk to me again. I'm just making sure we're on the same page."

Myrtle's discomfort must have shown on her face because Sherry interjected, "But plenty of people didn't like Jill. Blanche couldn't stand being in the same room with her. And Georgia Simpson absolutely hated her guts and told anybody that would listen. So I'm not the only one."

"And here I thought that Jill was this wonderful person who kept an immaculate house, volunteered her rear-end off, and put up beautifully with a difficult husband," Myrtle shook her head. "I guess I'm no judge of human nature. Why do you think Blanche and Georgia hated Jill so much?"

"I don't have a clue why Blanche was upset with Jill. Maybe Jill broke some of her Waterford crystal when she was cleaning her house?" Sherry gave a short laugh. "As far as Georgia, I think money was at the bottom of it. I saw Georgia giving Jill absolute hell a few months ago at the grocery store. Raving about Jill owing her money or something. Who knows? I'd have thought that Jill didn't have two cents to rub together. Maybe Georgia loaned Jill some money and was trying to get paid back."

Myrtle caught sight of Miles walking towards them. Typical, she thought. She was all done with the conversation now. "Well, here's Miles, so I better run. He's my walking buddy today."

"Have a nice walk then."

As Sherry got back to her weeds, Myrtle thumped over to Miles and hissed at him, "Thanks for being on time! I had no idea how terrified you were of Erma Sherman."

"You're not so brave, yourself, Myrtle. I've seen you pop your head back in your door if you catch the smallest glimpse of her. Did you find out what she was doing in Cullen's house this morning?"

Myrtle felt a flush of irritation. "No, actually, I didn't. I completely forgot to ask her. That Erma interruption threw me for a loop. Listen, I did manage to find some things out, though. Sherry couldn't stand Jill because she was too perfect. And she wants to make sure I'm her alibi for the murder."

Miles said slowly, "You weren't with her the whole party, were you?"

"No," said Myrtle, "I was actually trying to escape from her so that I could talk to Blanche and Georgia for a bit and see what was going on with them. But I did spend some time talking to Sherry at your house and at Willow's."

"But she wasn't there the whole time," said Miles. "I actually noticed she'd gone because I wanted to ask her something about the variety of Knock-Out rose that she has in her side yard. But I couldn't find her until right before it was time to leave Willow's house to head over to Jill's."

Myrtle absorbed this. "Sherry could have slipped out, hustled the short distance to Jill's house, killed Jill, and come back to Willow's to join our group before making the next stop."

"She was busily eating a tossed salad when I saw her," said Miles. "But do you really think Sherry would have murdered Jill? Being irritated at her perfectionism is one thing, but smashing her over the head with a cast-iron skillet then coolly eating a salad a few minutes later is something else."

"I don't know," said Myrtle glumly. "There have been many times when I've thought about killing Erma. I'm pretty sure I could do it in cold blood. And eat a salad afterward. Or maybe even a steak."

"Maybe Georgia did it," said Miles.

Myrtle only lifted her eyebrows. This is why Miles would never progress beyond sidekick status.

Miles continued, "Georgia hated Jill. Money came between the two friends and was tearing their relationship apart. It was eating Georgia alive. She obsessed over the money that was rightfully hers, day and night. Finally, she couldn't handle it any more. She stormed Jill's house and walloped her with the handy, cast iron skillet, finally avenging her financial loss."

Myrtle studied him. "How fanciful of you, Miles. I don't think I've ever heard you speak so melodramatically before. I can only assume that this means you are passionately in love with Georgia. You're fixated on her and have been since the first time you met her at the Kiwanis breakfast."

Miles colored. "I don't know what you're talking about."

"Georgia Simpson is the wild part of you, dying to be set free. The part that likes middle-aged women with poorly-dyed hair, tattoos, and too much mascara. She completes you!"

"Myrtle," said Miles forcefully. "Shut up."

Which, to Myrtle, only proved her point.

But she was gracious enough to move on. "When was she supposed to have killed Jill? Before or after she passed out at your house?"

"I think," said Miles, holding himself stiffly, "That she could have done it either time. I mentioned to you before that I thought she was capable of staggering over to Jill's and killing her. Murdering Jill wouldn't have taken all that much coordination since the frying pan was so big. Then she could have just stumbled on back to my house. Jill's house is just around the bend in the road. And with all the trees in this neighborhood, she could have walked through yards and no one would have even seen her. Besides, no one would have thought anything if they *had* seen her. Everyone was walking back and forth from one house to the next. Some people were even walking back to their houses to use their own restrooms before coming back to my house. I don't remember Georgia at the earring hunt or the subsequent glass cleanup."

Myrtle mulled this over. "That's true. But that could mean that she was already out cold. Let's say, just for argument's sake, that she passed out early in the evening. After she'd upset Blanche. She got a good little nap in, woke up, went to the bathroom perhaps, then wandered off to kill Jill. She returned to your house (while everyone was at Willow's house), finished up any leftover wine, and passed out again."

Miles quietly reflected on this scenario. "Does this mean it was premeditated? It sounds like she carefully picked a time to kill Jill when no one would be around."

"I can't see someone that sloshed being careful. No, I think she woke up, realized no one was there, stumbled over to Jill's house thinking that it was time for the barbeque part of the party, saw no one there but Jill (Cullen was probably passed out himself), flew into a drunken rage, and took advantage of the moment."

Miles nodded slowly.

"*If* she did it," said Myrtle. "Which I doubt." Sometimes, sidekicks needed to be put in their place.

Chapter Six

"That cat," Myrtle told Elaine, "is living the high life." Watching the cat eliminating the squirrel population had turned out to be great fun. She'd had to call Elaine to tell her about it. "She's hunting like a maniac, just for fun. Pigging out on dry cat food and tuna in my backyard. She's going to be one fat, happy kitty."

"Uh-oh. I think I forgot to explain something. There's more to the Friends of Ferals program."

"I thought you told me I should feed and water the cat and keep it outside and that was it!"

"No, no. Well, yes, you're supposed to feed and water it and leave it outside. But you've got to *capture* the cat first of all. Then I'll drive you and the cat to the vet that participates in the program and we'll get it spayed or neutered. *And* give it its shots. Because it could end up with rabies or something! You've got to protect yourself *and* the cat first."

Myrtle was stuck at *capture the cat*. "Capture the cat? Wait in the bushes with a bedspread? It all seems very cloak and dagger. She *trusts* me now."

Elaine said slowly, "Do you have feelings for the cat now, Myrtle? It sounds like ... "

"Of course not. This is a wild animal we're talking about. Undomesticated. It just seems like ... a dirty trick, that's all."

"I'm sure it won't hold it against you, Myrtle. You won't even be around when the cat is caught. Hold on, I'll come right over."

A few minutes later, Elaine was at Myrtle's house, equipment in tow. "This will be a piece of cake. We're just going to leave the food in the trap. The cat has gotten a few meals from you, so it should be easy-peasy getting her into the trap. She'll just think she's getting her usual meal. Then the trap will close and tomorrow morning we'll take her to the vet."

Late that night, when Myrtle's usual insomnia struck, she peeked out the kitchen window into the backyard. The food was gone and there was no cat in the trap. Myrtle smiled.

Myrtle did try to go back to sleep after checking the cat trap. But she couldn't stop thinking about the casserole dishes at Jill's house. Had Tippy made a note of the women from book club who'd signed up to help Jill out by bringing a side to supper club? All of those women would have dropped off food and been in Jill's house—all, obviously, before her murdered body lay on the floor. Except for the killer.

Myrtle peeked out the side window. Was Miles up, too? She checked the kitchen clock. Two a.m. It was her normal time for waking up, and Miles's too. She absently pulled on a long raincoat over her nightgown for decency's sake, took her cane from beside the door, and strolled out into the warm night.

Erma's lights were out, she noted with relief. All she needed was Miss Nosy charging out of her house and pointing a flashlight on her. When she got closer to Miles's house, she frowned. She couldn't really tell if his lights were on or not. There was sort of a dim light coming from one of the windows, but that could maybe be a light you'd leave on all night in the kitchen. Or a bathroom nightlight. Or ...

"Mama!" hissed beside her.

Myrtle jumped and whirled around to see Red glaring at her from his police car window. "Red!" she fussed. "You scared the living daylights out of me."

"Well, you're scaring *me,* floating around in the middle of the night like a ghost. What the devil are you doing out here at two a.m.?"

"What the devil are *you* doing out here at two a.m.?" asked Myrtle.

"I'm on patrol, Mama. Making sure Bradley's skillet killer isn't on a murdering rampage. Now what are *you* doing again?"

Myrtle fidgeted with the hem of her raincoat. "I'm just seeing if Miles's lights are on. Or out. I had this thought about the casserole dishes at Jill's house and wanted to ask him about it."

"I think *your* lights must be out. Now I know you like going on walks with your insomnia and all, but really—is this the safest time to be ambling around the neighborhood? A violent crime was just committed, not far from where you're standing. And it was most likely somebody you know, in this very neighborhood. There were plenty of opportunities for your wonderful supper club friends to slip away and murder Jill Caulfield." He sighed when he saw Myrtle's dejected look. "Why don't you get into the car and I'll drive you home."

"Red, I'm just two houses from home."

"Well, it doesn't look like your friend is awake. Please don't go waking him up in the middle of the night to talk to him about casserole dishes. Besides, you might trip yourself up with that long raincoat and nightgown. Let me at least get you to your front door."

Myrtle decided to give in. When Red was in one of his stubborn moods, there was no arguing with him. "Anyway, if you're well and truly awake and bored, I know something you could do."

Myrtle raised her eyebrows.

"Your helpful hints column. This is early Wednesday morning. Isn't your deadline nine a.m.?"

It was funny how the mere mention of the column had made her sleepy, thought Myrtle as she walked to the newspaper office the next morning. She'd fought the Sandman as she pulled tips from her email inbox and the mail she'd gotten during the week. She'd hit the sack with great relief after compiling the tips into article form and giving it a quick read-over. She'd definitely *not* wanted to get up when her alarm went off at eight.

She pushed open the old wooden door of the *Bradley Bugle* office and saw Sloan flitting from one paper-laden desk to another. If he was looking for something, it would have to be a needle in a haystack with all the paper and pictures stacked in the newsroom. Somehow, though, Sloan always managed to find what he was looking for.

"Miss Myrtle? Thank the good Lord you're here. Got a column for me? I'm desperate for content this week. I'm looking for some column I did a while back that maybe I can stick in as filler." Sloan lifted another pile of papers hopefully.

"How's that possible, Sloan? We had a murder in town this week—there should be gobs of content for you," said Myrtle.

Sloan made a big hushing sound and pointed his beefy arm towards the back of the newsroom. Now Myrtle saw Willow, listlessly pecking at a keyboard. Myrtle looked chagrined and Sloan drew closer and whispered, "Don't worry. I don't think she even registered that you came in. She's in a real state. I had to call her this morning and ask her to do the horoscopes. I figured, we need the content, she needs a distraction, right?"

"But *why* do you need more content?" Myrtle said under her breath.

"Well, the Good Neighbors column is taking a break this week because Emily is sick. And then the cooking column writer is on vacation. There's only so much I can put in about the murder because we don't really know anything. I hope to heaven that you took some pictures and wrote up that post on the supper club so we can have something on the blog. I've played up just about every angle I could possibly think of and it's pretty played out now." He clumsily patted Myrtle's arm.

She guiltily remembered that the pictures she'd unenthusiastically taken at the progressive dinner were probably not all that great. Besides, she wasn't even sure how to get them off her phone. Not to mention the helpful hints column. "I was about to forget about the column this week, myself. Red reminded me about it."

Sloan looked like he needed a Tums. "I don't even like *hearing* that, Miss Myrtle. That's all I'd need this week, another vacancy in the newspaper."

Myrtle said in a low voice, "If everything works out well, we could have a great story on our hands." Sloan frowned and Myrtle said, "The murder? I'm trying to do some detective work. Investigative journalism. You know."

"Detecting?" Now Sloan was too excited for even his stage-whisper. "That worked out great for us the last time, Miss Myrtle. The article was fantastic and the newsstands sold totally out of it. Remember that the state paper even picked it up on the AP wire?" Sloan puffed his chest out. "I'm putting you officially on assignment. But keep up with the helpful hints, too. And the blog. When you crack the case, give me the exclusive. Or, heck, write it yourself. We can use another story like that to boost circulation."

"I'll make a note of it," said Myrtle dryly. "In the meantime, here's my column. Maybe you can show some enthusiasm over it, too."

Sloan gave Myrtle a cautious smile. He was always a little nervous of her sarcasm or bad humor, having been familiar with both when she'd been his English teacher long ago. He'd never really gotten over the experience. He scanned the paper she handed him. "Uh, great stuff here. Love the tip about putting safflower seed in your birdfeeder to keep the squirrels away."

Myrtle peered closely at him to make sure he wasn't making fun of her. Satisfied, she nodded. "It's a good tip. There are plenty of birdwatchers in Bradley." A movement caught the corner of Myrtle's eye and she saw that Willow stood right beside her.

Myrtle still couldn't believe the change in Willow. Her clothes and hair seemed to droop and she looked like she had just grabbed something from her closet—or that she was wearing what she'd slept in. She didn't have a drop of makeup on, and she wasn't one of those people who could really go without makeup.

Sloan widened his eyes dramatically at Myrtle in sort of a get-a-load-of-Willow look before turning to Willow and saying with forced jocularity, "Got that horoscope done? Boy, you don't know what a relief that is. We'd have panic in the streets if folks didn't have the newspaper's astrological insights into the week ahead."

Willow just looked at him blankly, then handed him the sheets of paper. "Okay. I'll see you next week." She glanced at Myrtle with a look Myrtle couldn't really read, and then ambled out the office door.

Sloan gave Myrtle a little push. "You'd better go after her, Miss Myrtle. In the interests of crime-fighting and all. Maybe she can give you some clues. She'd probably point the finger at Cullen, of course. She's sure to, she couldn't stand him. Half her horoscopes warn of steering clear of thin Scorpio men. Go, go!"

Myrtle hurried out the door, thumping her cane as she went. But by the time she'd made it out onto the sidewalk, Willow had already gotten into her car and was driving away. Myrtle watched her car speed off. *Shoot!*

Her thoughts didn't get any cheerier when she spotted Red's police car. He pulled up next to her on the sidewalk and rolled down his window. "Chasing suspects down the street, Mama? Maybe Willow doesn't *want* to talk to you. Most people don't want people snooping around in their business, you know. You should stop poking around."

"I was just going to ask her something for newspaper business, Red," said Myrtle in a huffy voice. "I *am* a reporter, you know. And Sloan wants me to write a story about the case and do a little investigating."

"I'll have to have a talk with my old buddy Sloan," growled Red. He'd asked Sloan to get his mother a job at the newspaper to keep her busy and out of trouble. He thought she'd still be tinkering around with her helpful hints column instead of making the leap to investigative journalism.

Red was too late in his good intentions to talk to Sloan. With a story shortage on his hands and a deadline just hours away, Sloan suddenly got a brainstorm for an interesting piece. Anyone picking up at paper at the Piggly Wiggly next day would see "Octogenarian Myrtle Clover Investigates Murder for the *Bradley Bugle,*" on the very front page.

Chapter Seven

When Myrtle opened her door the next morning to get the paper, she was horrified to see a grinning Erma on her doorstep. "I was just about to knock!" she beamed, breathing noxious fumes into Myrtle's too-close face.

"Really?" asked Myrtle coldly. "Since I'm still just waking up, Erma, so maybe another ... "

"We'll have a nice cup of coffee," said Erma, already striding into Myrtle's house.

"I don't drink it."

"*Sure* you do! I've seen you drink it dozens of times."

"I don't *anymore*, though. My doctor recommended I stop." For some reason, Myrtle thought grimly, being around Erma always made her start lying through her teeth.

Erma stuck her head in Myrtle's fridge. "Okay. I'm easy. Here are two Cokes, so let's stick with that then." She popped them open and put them on Myrtle's kitchen table with its red-checkered tablecloth.

Erma was *always* like this. Always. She just *hijacked* your day.

"So, let's talk about the murder," said Erma in a salacious voice that Myrtle found entirely inappropriate. "I saw that story in the paper today, Myrtle. All about your investigative reporting and all. I've got some really good theories about Jill's murder. *Good* ones." She guzzled noisily from her Coke can.

"Erma, *what* are you talking about? What story—"

"I'm liking Tiny Kirk for this murder," said Erma decidedly.

Now Erma had Myrtle's attention. "Tiny? Why on earth would Tiny Kirk want to murder Jill? They didn't even know each other."

Erma looked affronted. "Sure they did. They were even at the same party together. And Tiny helped break up that fight between Jill and Willow."

Myrtle clucked. "That doesn't mean they knew each other. Tiny was the only person young enough and big enough at that party to separate them. Look, I *do* know who did it, okay? I know *exactly* who did it because I remembered something right after the murder. I just need to collect some evidence before I unveil the killer to Red."

"Don't you mean share it with the newspaper?" asked Erma. "You're supposed to be writing the story for them."

Myrtle got up and walked straight outside to wrest the slender newspaper from the gnomes. *Well-known Octogenarian Tackles Murder Investigation*. And the subtitle: *Bugle Investigative Reporter Myrtle Clover Hot on the Trail of a Killer*. Great. Sloan could always be counted on to take the sensational route when he was desperate for subscriptions. No chance of working undercover as a gossipy old lady now.

Irritably, she said to Erma, "So now you know. As soon as I get some evidence, I'll have this case all wrapped up for the police."

It was worth any little white lies to see Erma's face, gaping at her, thought Myrtle with satisfaction. Tiny Kirk! Tiny didn't have the brains to show *up* for a murder, much less orchestrate one.

"Oh. Okay. I'll see you at the visitation this afternoon then," said Erma, sounding for all the world like they were both going to be guests at a garden party. "Can't wait to hear who the killer is."

Jill's graveside funeral was closed to all but the family. Myrtle had a suspicion that this was because Cullen was too intoxicated for the town to witness him at his wife's funeral (and gossip about it later.) Instead, they had a visitation at the Gates of Heaven Funeral Home the morning before the funeral.

Cullen made an appearance for only a few minutes before one of his cousins drove him back home. Willow was there, wearing a black and brown caftan and with her white hair pulled back severely in a leather band. Cullen's brother, Simon, took his place and stood to greet visitors with his wife, Libba, beside him. He seemed coldly reserved, but dutiful.

Libba smiled appreciatively at everyone and looked as if she were itching to bring out food and beverages. She looked painfully aware that this was *not* the way she'd been brought up to do funerals in the South. In small towns like Bradley, it was still customary to have the visitation at the family home, not the funeral home. There should be a frantic day of cleaning to get the house company-ready, a dining room table groaning with Chicken Divan casseroles, and an army of church ladies bossing each other around.

"I'm so sorry," murmured Myrtle to Simon and Libba. "I really did like Jill."

They thanked her and Myrtle signed the guest book and walked out to the Gates of Heaven's front lobby. She was horrified to hear Erma Sherman's voice, at its usual high volume, "I'll never forget the sight of her, dead as a doornail on the kitchen floor. Such a shame about that barbeque, too. At least it wasn't a total waste, since we all helped ourselves to it. And soon we won't have to be barricading ourselves in our houses, either. Myrtle knows who did it! She said she's just collecting some evidence and then she'll get Red to lock him up."

Myrtle froze in horror as Red picked that very moment to walk out of the Caulfield's visitation room. His expression was stormy. Beside him was Willow, looking frozen.

"She just needs a little more evidence, you know. Can't turn somebody in without any evidence. But the murderer is sure to screw something up. The killer wasn't smart killing Jill like that, anyway. Blood everywhere! And supper club on its way over."

Finally someone in Erma's group caught a glimpse of Willow's usually-pale face now blotched with red at the mention of Jill's blood. "Shhh!" she said to Erma, who clapped a hand over her mouth. But Erma was determined to make the best use of the spotlight. "I was thinking it could be Georgia. You know? Because Georgia hated her guts. And she could have easily walked over to Jill's house from Miles's."

Willow spun around and scurried back into the visitation room. Elaine winced at the scene and looked questioningly at Myrtle. Myrtle just shrugged. She wasn't going to admit to anything. Not while Erma was being so unexpectedly interesting.

"Erma! For heaven's sake," said Tippy. "Georgia's just standing right over there!"

And she was. Glowering. "And I'm thinking I could save time by taking you out right here in a funeral home. Since there are caskets here and everything."

Miles looked intrigued.

Erma had the grace to blush an unbecoming shade. "Did I say *your* name? I meant that *Sherry* probably did it. She hated living next to Jill. Bad blood there, you know."

Myrtle was, by now, thoroughly enjoying herself. Erma was really very self-destructive today, which was unlike her. Sherry was standing right behind her ... until she moved around to shoot Erma a look that would freeze hell itself and stalked off.

Erma didn't look nearly as discomfited by the experience as an ordinary person would, but she wasn't as chatty as she usually was, either. After Erma started behaving herself, the visitation got a lot duller.

Tippy moved closer to Myrtle and murmured, "How *do* you stand living next door to her?"

"I'm a saint."

Tippy looked doubtfully at Myrtle and changed the subject. "I offered to pick up Willow and take her to the United Methodist Women luncheon tomorrow. The covered dish one? I thought it would be a good idea for her to get out of the house a little, since she's looking sort of puny. You mentioned at the supper club that you were interested in doing more with the UMW."

Tippy said this as a statement of fact. Myrtle winced. She must have said that during a lull in the conversation. She hated awkward little lulls. Tippy, as president of the United Methodist Women, would naturally be happy to capitalize on Myrtle's moment of weakness.

"So I hope we'll see you there tomorrow. It's a great little lunch and then we'll discuss business. We're really looking for members to join our Bereavement Visitation Casserole committee."

Myrtle nodded glumly. She'd expected as much.

Miles walked with Myrtle back to her house.

"Did I tell you," asked Myrtle, "how much I'm enjoying *The Master and Margarita*? I've been completely bowled over by it."

"Really." Miles folded his arms over his chest as he walked. "What was your favorite part of Bulgakov's book?"

"Oh, it's so hard to choose a favorite part with a book like that. With classic literature like *The Master and Margarita*, every bit plays like a finely tuned instrument."

"Did you like the part where Anthony renounced his family and embraced a nomadic existence, living solely on the kindness of strangers?" asked Miles.

"Now that you mention it, yes. Yes, I loved that part. It really exhibited his unique spirit and search for something important outside himself. Something absent in his life."

"Myrtle," said Miles in a grave voice, "I completely made that part up. There's not even an Anthony in the book. The book is a satire on atheist socialism and stifling bureaucracy in 1930s Moscow."

"Oh," said Myrtle. She suddenly felt very cross.

"What was it that you wanted? You might as well just come out with it."

"I'd like to borrow your car," said Myrtle.

Miles winced. He was as protective over that silly Volvo as an old biddy with her cat, thought Myrtle.

"Do you remember how to drive?" asked Miles in a halting voice.

Myrtle narrowed her eyes. "Of course I do, Miles! I drove a car for forty years. I could drive your car in my sleep."

"That's what I'm worried about! You said car rides make you sleepy."

"When I'm a *passenger*!" said Myrtle.

"Why don't I just drive you wherever it is that you want to go?"

Myrtle glared at him. "Because I don't want you coming along!" She gave him a huffy sigh. "I'm going to see a psychic. That's all. And she's a little skittish."

Miles just stared at her. "A psychic?"

"Don't get all superior on me. You know very well that there were psychics even in Atlanta. And this one has reliable information sometimes. Her name is Wander."

"Wander?" said Miles, tasting the unfamiliar name on his tongue.

"Wanda, I guess. But her brother calls her Wander." Miles still looked hesitant and Myrtle said impatiently, "She's someone I met during my last case—she lives out in the sticks with her brother, Crazy Dan. This might sound crazy, but I think she might have Powers."

Miles squinted doubtfully at the word Powers. "Welllll ... all right. But please make sure I don't end up regretting this."

Myrtle's trek to the psychic took her down an old rural highway lined with decaying motels and ivy-infested buildings. Before the interstate system, Myrtle remembered the road had been a bustling thoroughfare. Now no one really hopped on the road unless there was construction or an accident on the interstate that they were desperate to avoid.

There weren't many houses out there. Except for Crazy Dan's. And Crazy Dan and Wander weren't the kind to embrace change. A rotten sign proclaiming "CRAZY Dan's Boil P-nuts, Hubcaps, Fireworks, Live Bait!!!" was next to another decrepit sign with a palm and "Madam Zora, Sykick" barely visible. Myrtle pulled off down the dirt driveway into Crazy Dan's yard. She took out her cane and walked carefully to the house, avoiding tree roots sticking out of the red clay.

The last time she'd come by Crazy Dan's tiny house, she'd puzzled over announcing her arrival. The shack was completely covered by hubcaps. Even the front door. And there was no doorbell. This time she didn't hesitate before lifting up her cane and rapping it forcefully against one of the metal hubcaps.

Crazy Dan opened the door and stuck his grizzled face out. His face was nearly covered too—by a wild, mangy beard and shaggy gray hair. "You agin!" As if it'd been mere hours instead of months. "What'cha want this time?"

The man was the worst salesman in the history of the world, thought Myrtle crossly. You'd think, if someone *actually* drove down that rural highway and *actually* became interested by the weather-beaten sign and *actually* cared enough to show up at your tin can of a house, then you'd have your best sales face on. "I want," she said, testing the waters, "some live bait."

Crazy Dan's eyes squinted at her in his leathery face. "What for?"

"To catch fish with, what else? Your sign promises live bait."

He expertly spat a stream of tobacco at the base of a pine tree. "Ain't got none."

"How about a hubcap then? You've got plenty of those." Myrtle nodded toward his house.

"Can't. House'd fall in if I take one of 'em off."

"Never mind. What I really came for is Wanda. I need some psychic advice. She's here, isn't she?" Myrtle was pretty sure that Wanda was *always* there. The cars in the dirt yard were all set up on cinder blocks and appeared to have broken down at some point in the 1980s, judging from the models.

A shrewd look passed over his wizened face. Money was sure to be at the bottom of that look. Probably already wondering if he could get Myrtle to be a frequent client of Wanda's. Then he could replace whatever part had gone bad in one of those old heaps and escape from the shack every once in a while.

"Wander? I mean, Madam Zora? Yeah, she's here. Lemme run git 'er. You kin git yer fortoon outside."

That was fine with Myrtle. She'd gone inside the hubcap house last time and had no desire to repeat the experience. A minute later, Crazy Dan returned with a crone that was, except for the scraggly beard and hopefully a few other parts, an exact replica of Crazy Dan himself. He also carried a decrepit rocking chair that Myrtle gathered she was to sit in. Wanda put down a stepstool in front of her and looked gravely at her.

"Yer still alive," she said in a gravelly, cigarette-damaged voice. "I'm amazed."

Myrtle felt the same chilly frisson course down her spine that she'd felt the last time when Wanda had told her she was in danger. "Still here," she said, trying to sound perky. Wanda just stared at her with those intense eyes.

"And yer still runnin' after death." There was a ring of condemnation to the words.

Myrtle shifted uncomfortably in the rocking chair. Her discomfort stemmed as much from the broken frame jutting through the cushion as it did from Wanda's disapproval. "This time it was someone I *liked*," she offered in defense. "A girl who cleaned for me. Her time was cut too short. I wanted to see what you could tell me about it."

"Well, *he* didn't do it. The one yer wantin' ter talk to."

"Cullen?"

"He's feelin' right guilty. And he weren't the one."

The husband usually *was* the one who'd murdered his wife. And she couldn't see Cullen feeling guilty at all. Maybe Madam Zora really was a fraud, after all.

Wanda's leathery face looked drawn and tired. "Go ahead and talk to 'im, then. I know you will, no matter what I say."

Myrtle reached in her pocketbook for money, but Wanda shooed a bony hand at her in irritation. "Yer puttin' yerself in danger again. Don't want nuthin' to do wid it."

Just like last time, Madam Zora's words served to put Myrtle in a very bad mood. She wasn't fond of being warned off. And she'd been wanting, in her heart of hearts, to pin Jill's murder on Cullen. Cullen had been horrible to Jill and deserved *some* kind of retribution. He made the most *sense* as a murderer. Georgia seemed way too intoxicated to have killed Jill. Would Sherry actually kill over a noisy Christmas display? When it wasn't even Christmas? Willow was angry at Jill, it was true—but she was angrier at *Cullen*. If *Cullen* had been the victim, then maybe she'd suspect Willow more. And Blanche just seemed like she wanted to stay out of Jill's way—it didn't seem possible that she'd deliberately go confront Jill.

So it had to be Cullen. Didn't it? Myrtle knew Wanda was just a sham. But she couldn't explain the uneasy feeling she got that Cullen really wasn't the right direction for her to follow.

Taking a little ride would shake off this foreboding feeling. Back in the day, nothing had been able to take her mind off her troubles faster than a ride in the car. And lucky her—here she was with a perfectly serviceable, *red* Volvo at her disposal. She'd head to the town square and wave like she was in a parade. Because what was the joy in a joyride without people seeing you having fun?

Myrtle rolled the windows down and drove around the town square, honking as she went. Maisy Perry jumped half a mile and almost dropped her pocketbook. Myrtle spotted Red and waved gaily out the window of the Volvo as he glared. She even tooted the horn at Erma, who'd no doubt be gleefully spreading all kinds of stories about Myrtle since she was driving Miles's car. She even tooted the horn at Cullen when she saw him, killer or not. Then she pulled up to the curb that Cullen was staggering off of.

"Need a ride, Cullen?" she hollered out the window at him.

And got her chance to test out Madame Zora's prediction.

Chapter Eight

Unfortunately, taking Cullen home was something like a thirty second drive. Fortunately, Cullen was wasted enough not to notice that Myrtle drove around the square four or five times so she could talk to him a little longer.

"I'm glad to get a chance to tell you, Cullen, how sorry I was about Jill. You might not know it, but she'd started cleaning for me and my house had never been that clean. Not ever."

Cullen made a snuffling sound. "She was a good girl," he said in a low voice.

"She did everything well, didn't she? Your yard was always the neatest one on the street. And she cooked really well I hear—I've heard the old ladies at the church bragging on her and they hadn't been impressed with anyone's cooking since their mamas'."

The snuffling was louder this time. "Her red beans and rice were to die for."

An unfortunate choice of words.

Cullen continued. "I feel horrible about it Miss Myrtle. Can't sleep. Can't eat. Don't want to see anybody. I wasn't a good husband to Jill and now it's too late to say I'm sorry. I'm a sorry excuse for a husband."

Myrtle was about to ask if there was any *other* reason he might feel guilty about Jill—-like if he'd killed her, for instance. She started the car another lap around the square when Red pulled her over in his patrol car. With his lights, siren, and everything. Pooh.

"License and registration, ma'am," said Red grimly.

Myrtle crossly rooted around in her pocketbook. "Here's the license. I'm about to get it renewed so that it's good through 2026."

Red seemed not to like the thought of his mother terrorizing the Bradley populace in 2026.

"And the registration, ma'am? Is this car registered in your name or is it a stolen vehicle?"

She made a face at him. "I suppose Miles stuck his registration in the glove compartment. Hold on a minute." She reached across Cullen, who had unfortunately fallen asleep, and fumbled around in the glove box until she'd found the registration.

"You know you were speeding, Mama?"

"I was going thirty miles an hour!"

"Speed limit is fifteen around the square."

"Shoot! Are you giving me a ticket? *Sharper than a serpent's tooth ...*"

"I'm not a thankless child and you're not King Lear. I may let you off with a warning."

"Cullen?" Red woke Myrtle's sleeping passenger. "Are you ready to go home?"

Cullen nodded and Red said, "I don't think Cullen wants to go around and around the square all day while you interrogate him, Mama. So unless you take him straight home, I'll have to consider a kidnapping charge."

Myrtle glared at him. "I'm on my way back to Cullen's house now. And I wasn't interrogating him—we were having a conversation and I was offering my sympathies."

Red looked at Cullen, dozing again and hardly likely to dispute Myrtle's version of events. "I've got to get home anyway," she said with a sniff. "I've got to get ready for the United Methodist Women's luncheon."

Red looked more doubtful about Myrtle's sudden desire to go to church than he had about the non-interrogation.

The United Methodist Women's luncheon would be a good opportunity to talk to a few of the slipperier suspects. Like Willow, who'd successfully eluded her last attempt at questioning her. Willow had espoused many different ideas on religion in Myrtle's presence before and seemed to have formed an amalgam of different ones she liked from Buddhism, Hinduism, Taoism, and Christianity. Tarot cards were thrown in there somewhere, too. Since there wasn't a place in Bradley, North Carolina, that shared her exact religious views, she was making-do at the Methodist church.

Myrtle heard Elaine's light tap on the horn. She grabbed her cane in one hand and opened her front door. And stopped in her tracks at the sight of a half-eaten cardinal corpse on her front doorstep. Myrtle glanced around for the perpetrator. The cat was lying near the bushes in a sunbeam, lazily watching her. Myrtle sighed. She'd have to get the shovel out later and move the little carcass.

She carefully stepped over the cardinal. As she got into Elaine's minivan, she said, "There's a bloody body on my doorstep, Elaine."

"What? That's great news, Myrtle! You've really made a feral friend. She's giving you presents to show how much she appreciates you."

"How can I tell her I'd appreciate it more if she *didn't* give me any more little gifts? Although I've got a little fondness for the creature, I'll admit. How do you think she got out of that trap without setting it off? Smart thing."

"I get this feeling," said Elaine in a carefully even voice, "that you're rooting for the cat, Myrtle. That a part of you is really pleased by the fact that she's escaping the trap."

Myrtle shook her head but looked away guiltily.

"We've really got to get her fixed, you know. Otherwise she's going to end up populating Bradley with feral kittens. And then we'll have to trap all of *them* in your back yard."

"Yes, all right, I know," said Myrtle crossly. "It's not like I'm helping with a jail break, Elaine. She's smart. She's outthinking us. But no, I don't want a bunch of little feral cats in my yard. We'll keep trying."

Jack made one of those sudden, bellowing baby noises that toddlers sometimes make out of the blue. Myrtle turned to smile at Jack in the back seat and he gummily grinned back at her from his car seat. "I was sure to tell Red today," said Myrtle in a serious tone, "that I *do* attend community events of my own volition. Maybe you could remind him again later today. He doesn't have to stick his nose into my business because I have plenty going on."

Elaine knew that was precisely what worried Red. It was *what* Myrtle had going on that was the problem. Elaine felt pretty certain that Myrtle's motive for attending the United Methodist Women luncheon was complicated and had little to do with joining committees or church fundraising.

"It's always wonderful to spend time at the church," said Myrtle piously. "So vital for those of us with little time left, you know."

This was news to Elaine. She'd offered to take Myrtle to church with them the last few months to no avail.

"And it will be good to spend time with other believers, of course."

Ah, thought Elaine. Now we come to the true reason why Myrtle was interested in going to the luncheon. "You think certain believers are likely to be there?" asked Elaine.

Myrtle's look was cutting. "If you're talking about Sherry, Blanche, and Willow, yes, I'm hoping they'll be there. After all, they need spiritual nourishment after the rough week they've had with Jill's death. And it might be helpful for them to talk to others about their feelings," ended Myrtle in a self-righteous tone.

Elaine felt a giggle tickling up her throat. Myrtle would never forgive her if it sneaked out. Fortunately, the church was only a few blocks away and they were already pulling into a parking place.

The dining hall was full of ladies of various ages, old and young. Myrtle took a peek at the buffet line and made a face. It was a hot lunch, but the offerings looked suspect and the broccoli casserole looked soupy. She brightened at the glasses of iced tea at each placemat, though. The church did have good sweet tea.

As she had hoped, the ladies she'd wanted to see there *were* there. Blanche was already sitting at a table and talking to some of Bradley's other society matrons. Tippy and Sherry were talking to each other near the buffet line and Willow stood morosely nearby.

Elaine leaned in to whisper, "I saw Tippy picking Willow up earlier. I think she thought it would be good for her to get out of the house."

"Tippy mentioned it to me at the visitation. I guess Willow is her new cause." Myrtle squinted across the room. "Why is Willow bringing her own food?" asked Myrtle.

"Oh, she's a vegetarian."

"Aren't there veggies here?" Myrtle frowned over at the buffet table in the direction of the soupy broccoli.

"All the veggies were prepared by Southern cooks, you know. Cooked in gravy and bacon grease."

"That's right, she's one of those clean-living nuts," muttered Myrtle. "When she abandoned us during supper club, I was rooting around in her fridge and saw a bunch of organic stuff in there."

"She certainly seems to be a health nut. But I was shocked yesterday when I saw her buy a pack of cigarettes at the gas station. It just didn't seem to gel with her image."

Myrtle shrugged. "You know how hippies are," she said. "Or maybe it's just the stress of losing her sister that made her pick up a bad habit again."

Willow wasn't looking her best. Again. This time she wasn't even looking particularly clean. She looked to be giving one-word answers to Sherry's attempts to include her in conversation, and Myrtle saw Sherry and Tippy shrug at each other. They saw Myrtle and waved.

"Want to go ahead and find a place to sit down?" asked Elaine.

Myrtle quickly chose a table in the middle of the dining hall in the hopes of being close to *somebody* there. She hung her bulky bag and her cane on the back of a chair and she and Elaine walked over to the buffet line.

It took a while to navigate through the line. Apparently some of the older ladies had a hard time choosing between the meatloaf and turkey and gravy. Or the broccoli and rice or green beans. Myrtle impatiently drummed her fingers against her plastic tray. Elaine seemed to be hovering in case the caneless Myrtle started to sway. Myrtle couldn't decide if that was annoying or endearing.

She was horrified to see Erma Sherman bulldoze through the throng of church members. Erma bellowed, "Myrtle! Good to see you at the square this morning—driving Miles's car around. I hadn't seen you go out of your house this morning and you know I always worry that you're lying on the floor with a broken hip."

Sherry, who had just filled her plate, winced sympathetically at Myrtle as she joined Blanche and Willow off to a table that already had people sitting there. Shoot.

Erma gave an enormous cough, primly covering her mouth with her hands but neglecting to think about transferring germs before grabbing Myrtle's hand. "Since there's a murderer wandering around killing people, I was worried he'd got you! I was all set to break into your house after the luncheon and make sure your throat wasn't slit or something. Good thing I saw you in yours and Miles'scar."

Myrtle shuddered and made a mental note to add a chain to her door. She ignored the snide reference that Miles and she had joint ownership over large purchases. Murderers she could handle ... Erma Sherman was something else. She broke away from Erma as soon as possible, carefully made her way to her table, and then made a beeline for the ladies' room to wash up.

By the time she got back from the restroom, a lot of the ladies were still milling around. It seemed to take forever for anything to get accomplished at the United Methodist Women with all the visiting that transpired. This was a major reason that Myrtle ordinarily didn't frequent these meetings and luncheons. But visiting ... .and gossiping ... was exactly why she was there today. Unfortunately, she and Elaine weren't at the best place to do much of that. They were at a table with a couple of church ladies Myrtle didn't know, as well as Tippy Chambers and Maisy Perry, Willow's predecessor for the horoscope. Maisy was looking a little better than she had when she'd come down with her case of nerves. Myrtle still had hope that Blanche or Willow would come over to talk.

Maisy Perry was the poster child for nervousness. Her cadaverous body trembled constantly, and her eyes stared out through her huge glasses in unblinking horror at all the world showed her. When she talked, she fluttered her thin hands around so that she looked like a little bird trying to take flight. Myrtle sighed. Spending time with Maisy was enough to make Myrtle feel jumpy herself.

Myrtle poked her broccoli and rice and looked over at Blanche, Sherry, and Willow's table, while Maisy explained why she'd needed a break from the *Bradley Bugle* and the grueling life of horoscope manufacturing.

Myrtle tuned back into the conversation when she realized Elaine was trying to get her attention. "Maisy was wondering what you thought of Willow's horoscopes, Myrtle."

Myrtle looked at Elaine and Maisy blankly. "I haven't read them. Sorry. I don't have enough hours in my day to spend time dabbling in the occult."

Elaine groaned and Maisy said eagerly, "Oh, it's not the dark arts at all, Miss Myrtle. I know it seems like a whole lot of mystical stuff going on, but God created the stars, didn't he? So he shouldn't mind us reading the signs they're giving us. Maybe they're even signs from God himself!"

Now the conversation had shifted to other supernatural things like Ouija boards and "light as a feather, strong as a board" while Myrtle gloomily looked for an escape route. Maybe she could come up with an excuse to visit another table. At that moment, however, Maisy had gotten herself so wound up that she had a coughing fit. Since Maisy was the only person at the table without a drink, Myrtle pushed her own, untouched iced tea over.

Maisy took a few big gulps, stopped coughing ... then started choking while her table watched in horror. Maisy seemed unable to breathe, grabbing at her throat with clawing hands, face turning purple. At first, everyone at the table sat in stunned silence. Then a woman from the next table, who was a nurse, lunged over yelling, "Call 911!"

It felt almost like a dream as the ambulance arrived and the medics rushed back out, carrying Maisy out on a stretcher before the ambulance raced off again.

On the way home, Elaine said, "That was horrible, Myrtle. Maisy looked like she was in such agony. Isn't it odd it came over her so quickly? She'd been *fine* except for that coughing fit she was having."

She was fine until she had my iced tea. But the idea seemed too paranoid to voice. Besides, she didn't want Elaine to start wondering if she might be in danger. Then Red would be sure to stick to her like Super Glue.

"I guess sometimes these things hit you really fast," said Myrtle in a doubtful voice as they reached her driveway.

Elaine reached under the seat and pulled out a plastic grocery bag. "Here's a can of top-notch tuna, Myrtle. A cat's dream come true. Surely this will tempt the cat and make her hang out in the trap for long enough to trip it. I'll come back early tomorrow morning and take her to the vet."

The next morning the tuna was gone and so was the cat.

Chapter Nine

Myrtle spent much of the night thinking about Maisy. She called Elaine as early as decently possible the next morning, broke the news that the cat had stolen the tuna, then started right in with some questions.

"Did Red find out what happened to Maisy? What does Red know about it? How is she feeling? Is she still in the hospital? Does she need someone to bring her a casserole?"

Elaine shuddered on the other end of the phone. She had a feeling that Maisy, who had just recently undergone horrific gastric distress, would *not* want a Myrtle Clover casserole.

"She's still in the hospital, Myrtle. After all, she wasn't in the strongest of conditions even *before* she got sick. And Red mentioned ... " Elaine hesitated, but knew Myrtle would end up pulling it out of her. Red shouldn't give her information about his cases! He knew she couldn't keep a secret from Myrtle. " ... he mentioned that Maisy was poisoned. I don't know with what."

"What?" asked Myrtle with a sinking sensation in her stomach.

"Which is *ridiculous*! I mean, like anyone would want to poison poor little Maisy! Did someone put something in her green bean casserole? Really!"

Myrtle suddenly felt something very large and hard in her throat that made it hard to talk around. Nobody would want to murder Maisy. No one. But Myrtle? Maybe. And it was Myrtle's iced tea that Maisy had been drinking.

This was something that Elaine didn't need to know. Because this was something that *Red* didn't need to know. Apparently no one had noticed that it had been *Myrtle's* drink that Maisy had drunk from. Red was keeping close enough tabs on her as it was. If she wanted to make sure he wasn't going to stick one of those electronic surveillance ankle bracelets on her, she'd better just keep her trap shut.

There was a light tap on Myrtle's door. She peeped out the window, saw Miles, and said, "Elaine, I've got to run. Miles is here."

She opened the door. "Come on in, Miles," she said.

Miles's face looked oddly green. "There's a mangled rabbit on your front porch."

Myrtle leaned out the door and looked. She shrugged. "Just step over it for now. I'll get the shovel in a little while."

Miles skirted the small corpse, found a spot on Myrtle's sofa and said, "Myrtle? *Why* is there a dead rabbit on your front porch?"

"The cat," said Myrtle. She waved her hand impatiently at Miles's questioning face. "You know, the feral cat. It's just thanking me for feeding it."

"No good deed goes unpunished," said Miles. He looked intently at Myrtle's living room window. "I'm guessing that's the culprit there?"

Myrtle craned her head and saw the scrawny, black cat staring at them through the window. "The very one."

"Nobody's pretty child, is it?"

Myrtle surprised herself by feeling affronted. "She's had a hard life, Miles. You'd look the same if you poked around garbage cans looking for food."

"Have you named it?" he asked. "I'm thinking 'Fluffy' won't do."

"Not unless I'm being ironic. No, I need something tough, steely. Maybe something Russian. Pasha."

Miles nodded slowly. "Strong, yet feminine. And doesn't Pasha mean 'passion' in Russian? She definitely has a passion for slaughtering and disemboweling small, furry creatures."

Myrtle was cross. "How do you know so much trivia? How could you possibly know any Russian?"

"I read," said Miles loftily. He shifted in his seat. "You know, Pasha is making me uncomfortable just glowering at me. Is there something she wants from you?"

"Oh, who knows? She probably wants to hear a few 'good girls' from me for the rabbit. And the cardinal earlier." Myrtle looked thoughtfully at the cat and it opened its mouth for a silent meow. "I think I'll bring Pasha inside for a couple of minutes. Just to tell her what her name is."

Miles blinked. "You're not looking for a pet, are you?"

Myrtle stood up in an abrupt motion. "Of course not. I've got enough going on without having a live-in companion. I'm just curious to see what would happen if I brought her inside."

"Aren't feral cats completely unadoptable? And unpredictable around people?"

"Okay, *Elaine*. I'm not inviting Pasha in for good, just for a couple of minutes. She did go out of her way to slaughter offerings for me, after all." She turned the door knob, stuck her head outside, and called, "Here, kitty, kitty. Here, Pasha!"

There was the flash of black that was Pasha in motion. Myrtle turned to smile smugly at Miles for Pasha's obedience and obvious intelligence (A feral cat coming when called? What an amazing animal!). The smile died when she saw that Pasha was hissing dementedly and had attached herself to Miles's body like a clawed, fanged limpet.

Miles gave a high-pitched scream that Myrtle wouldn't have believed he could make and frantically tried peeling Pasha off of him. But Pasha was a virago, and determined to punish Miles for some unknown crime.

"Bad kitty! Bad Pasha! No!" said Myrtle.

"Get it oooooofffff meee!" yelled Miles.

Myrtle grabbed her glass of ice water and threw it on Pasha's back. And Miles's leg, of course, since that's where most of Pasha was. Pasha launched off of Miles, slinking to the corner of Myrtle's living room, and staring sulkily at Myrtle before licking her wet fur with emphatic strokes of her tongue.

Miles stood up shakily, summoning as much dignity as he could muster after being attacked by a stray cat in a friend's house. "I think I should go," he said coldly.

Myrtle bit the inside of her lip. She couldn't show any sign of the amusement that she was feeling over the whole situation or that would make him even angrier. "I'm sorry, Miles. I don't know what got into her. Maybe she was abused by a man at some point?"

"But *not*," said Miles, "by me. I'm sure Pasha can make the distinction between me and some cat abusing man." He sounded quite offended that the cat could have made such an error when determining the direction of his moral compass.

"I'm sorry, Miles," Myrtle repeated. "Uh ... what did you come over here to tell me to begin with? Before being ambushed, I mean."

Miles peered suspiciously at Myrtle, as if suspecting she might be laughing at him. "I wanted to let you know that I heard from the checkout lady at the grocery store that Willow and Jill had a huge argument in the store right before Jill was murdered."

"And she had that huge fight with Jill the night of the supper club, too. Willow's always been upset that Jill married Cullen and that she continued supporting him after he quit working. Was that the argument?"

Miles still looked pretty miffed. "If it was, it was the loudest, most animated argument about Cullen that they've had yet. That's what the checkout lady said."

Myrtle knit her brows. "I really want to find out some more information about Cullen. He seems to be at the very center of everything, but I really don't know much about him. I taught him, of course, but that was ... well, it was a while back. And Cullen doesn't seem like he's sober enough to hold an intelligent conversation. Maybe I could have a little chat with Simon, instead, and pick his brain about his brother. I wonder how I could make it seem like I've just casually run into him."

Miles pushed his glasses up and thought. "Actually, *I* know where he goes three times a week and exactly the time of day he's there."

"Please don't tell me it's the gym. I just told off Red a couple of weeks ago for trying to boss me into going over there. I made the mistake of telling Elaine that my doctor recommended I work out and she felt *compelled* to share that tidbit with Red."

"It's the gym. He's there Monday, Wednesday, and Friday during his lunch hour at noon. On the weight machines," added Miles helpfully. "Of course, even if you make it look casual, I'm sure he'll know why you're asking about his brother. Front page news, remember? Octogenarian sleuth?"

Myrtle blew out a deep breath. "True. But it's possible he doesn't even subscribe to the paper. That's why Sloan is feeling so desperate right now, after all. I guess I could go to the gym just the one time. For the sake of the case."

"You'll have to go over there more than once, Myrtle. The staff has to give you special training on using the machines so that you don't hurt yourself. Or the machines. What is it that your doctor told you you're supposed to be doing?"

"Building up bone mass," said Myrtle gloomily. "He said I was in fantastic shape, then completely contradicted himself by telling me to do some gentle weight lifting. And then Elaine was a blabbermouth and told Red what the doctor said. If Red has his way, I'll work out so much I'll be an Arnold Schwarzenegger look-alike."

"Not with the kind of workout you'd be doing, Myrtle. Besides, this gym isn't some body-building hangout. It's mostly middle-aged and older people trying to stay healthy. You might find that you really like it."

Miles eyed Pasha with apprehension as she seemed to grow restless and swished her tail a few times. "I'm ready to go now. I don't want to start round two with your new pet."

After receiving training on the equipment Thursday, Myrtle went into Fit Life shortly before noon on Friday. She scanned her membership card at the front desk and was surprised to see Sherry there. "I didn't know you worked here."

Sherry was digging out some membership paperwork for a new member and gave Myrtle a quick smile and said, "You probably wouldn't, unless you came here. I've seen Chief Clover here, of course."

Myrtle made a face. "He's been trying to get me here for weeks."

Sherry opened her mouth to respond, then clamped it shut before mumbling, "Excuse me, Miss Myrtle," and redirecting her attention to the new member. Myrtle turned around and saw Cullen Caulfield swaggering up to the desk. He worked out? Since when? He wasn't exactly trying to take care of himself. He seemed to be in no hurry to scan a membership card. Was he there for some other reason? Maybe to talk to Sherry? She remembered again the way Sherry had looked out from Cullen's window the morning after Jill's murder.

Myrtle decided that a cup of coffee from the coffee station in the lobby would be perfect before her workout. And a perfect excuse to stand around and see what happened.

But nothing seemed to be going to happen. Sherry appeared determined to pretend that Cullen was not there. She made herself busy with the new member, then settled down to filing applications and inputting the data on a computer. All the time, Cullen loped around the lobby, watching Sherry all the tim. Finally he leaned across the membership desk and bellowed, "Sherry! You're going to talk to me. I'm not going away."

Myrtle squeezed her coffee cup, nearly crushing the Styrofoam.

Sherry pretended that she hadn't heard anything and continued typing on the computer. Another employee walked out of the office, looking at Cullen curiously.

"Can I help you?" she asked, and Cullen shook his shaggy head, impatiently. "Are you a member here?" persisted the employee.

Just when Myrtle was sure Cullen was on the verge of being unceremoniously kicked out of the health club, things became even more interesting when Cullen's brother, Simon Caulfield, came through the door. Unlike his brother, Simon was clearly outfitted for exercising, and carried a workout bag as well.

Cullen and Simon looked like twins, even though they were several years apart. They both had a wasted quality about them: Cullen ... well, because he probably *was* wasted, and Simon because he looked like someone who wasn't happy with what he was doing in life. They were both tall, thin, angular, and serious.

Simon, his body stiff and face furious, said something quietly to Cullen. Cullen clenched his fists and said something in return that Myrtle couldn't catch. Myrtle crept closer to listen in. She was worried at first that they were going to find somewhere private to argue—but soon realized that they were angry enough to forget that anyone else was around.

"You killed her!" Cullen said in a vicious voice. "It was you, it must have been. You hated Jill."

"I hated the fact that she was sponging off of you with Dad's money! That money should have been mine. And then you drank the money, instead of doing anything useful with it at all. If *I'd* had that money ... "

"Oh *right*. Because if *you'd* had Dad's money, you'd be a Nobel Prize winner. Right. Same old story."

Simon stood very still. "I would have made something out of myself. Dad didn't mean for his money to be spent on booze," he said. "And it would kill him that your wife was cleaning other people's houses. There's no excuse for the way you've been just bumming around the house, drinking, while your wife works two jobs to scrape together a paycheck. What kind of man are you? She was scrubbing our toilets last week."

"It was the old man's money," said Cullen, ignoring Simon's mention of Jill's housekeeping. "He could do whatever the hell he wanted to with it. So he did. He didn't like your lifestyle ... "

"There *wasn't* any lifestyle," said Simon in a very quiet voice. "Lies. You lied to the old man to get his money. And somehow he believed you. And now you're trying to pin Jill's murder on *me*? You didn't give a rip about Jill."

"I *did*," said Cullen. His hands were clenched in fists at his side.

"Really? Because I'm thinking you got rid of her so you could mess around with ... "

Cullen gaped at his brother. "You think I *killed* her? She cooked for me. Cleaned for me. Did my yard work. Are you nuts?"

How touching, thought Myrtle. Really, he was just in the same position she was in with Puddin and Dusty—he hadn't wanted to lose his housekeeper and yard man.

"Besides, you couldn't stand Jill, either. And nobody knows what you were doing when she was killed. I've got a good idea ... I think you murdered her."

Simon gave a short laugh. "Why would I do that, Cullen? For what possible reason?"

"Plenty of them. You've always been embarrassed by Jill. You thought she wasn't good enough for our family. And maybe ... I think she figured out why Dad cut you out of the will. Maybe she didn't want to hold her tongue like I always have."

Now Simon's eyes were coldly furious. "There's nothing to find out. You made it all up. I didn't go near Jill. And get off your high horse, Cullen. If you'd cared anything about Jill then you wouldn't have been cheating on her right up until she died."

Myrtle's eyebrows shot up. She looked around to see if Sherry were listening and what her reaction was, but apparently Sherry had retreated to the back of the gym.

"Just because I cheated on her doesn't mean I didn't love her," said Cullen in what Myrtle considered a staggering lack of logic. "The affair didn't mean anything. Jill and I understood each other."

"It sure would've been *convenient* if Jill had been taken out of the way. Then there would have been nothing standing in the way of you two," said Simon. "How can you handle living in this town where everybody knows what a lazy, no-good guy you are? You had *plenty* of money. I heard about that windfall. But you were still happy to have Jill out there working like a dog."

And that was the moment when Cullen threw the first punch. Myrtle suddenly heard Red's voice bellowing out, "All right. *All right*! That's enough. Break it up, you two," and her son quickly strode into the lobby, reaching down a big hand to yank apart the brothers.

It only took a second for Cullen and Simon to separate. They stared at each other, panting. "Cullen, I know your sorry hide doesn't have a gym membership here. Get out before I charge you with trespassing. Simon, you better start exercising before you're charged with public fighting and disturbing the peace." Red waited while Cullen slunk out and Simon, still bristling, grabbed his workout bag and stalked into the weight room.

Red finally noticed Myrtle standing to the side, clutching her coffee. "Mama? What are you doing here?" he squinted suspiciously at her. "You always turn up like a bad penny whenever there's trouble. Should I be looking around for a dead body?" He did double take as he took in Myrtle's athletic outfit. "You're here to work out?"

Red's delight made Myrtle steam. She hated having him think he'd won that argument. But it would be worse having him think she was snooping around on his case. "Miles got me to go. He's been talking up this place for months. So I figured, why not? I didn't mind so much if I had somebody to exercise with me."

"Well, I'm just glad to see you here, Mama, whatever the reason was. You've been trained on the equipment and everything?"

"Yes, some man yesterday showed me how to use it. You know, I didn't see Sherry here yesterday. I didn't even know she worked here."

Red hoisted his workout bag back onto his shoulder. "Yeah, I usually see her in here when I come. She doesn't work every day, though."

"It's a good thing you were here when *you* were, Red. Considering that fight."

Red rolled his eyes. "Those two just don't get along. You'd think that brothers would have more in common. Seems like I break up a fight between those two every few months."

Myrtle trod carefully. She wanted to try and get information from Red, especially since she sensed he'd been knocked off-guard by her sudden interest in exercising. But she didn't want to supply him with any information he didn't already have. "It sounded to me," she said slowly, "like they were fighting over money. Like Simon was upset that their father had cut him out of his will and given the money to Cullen."

"Well, if that's what they were fighting about, it sure isn't the first time," snorted Red. "You'd think they'd stop going round and round on that subject. Cullen pressed charges years ago against Simon after the will was read and Simon jumped on him. Sounds like nothing much has changed. Do you remember how they were when they were boys?"

Myrtle said, "It wasn't too bad at the school because they were in different grades. But I remember a couple of times I heard about fights on the school bus." She snapped her fingers. "Almost forgot. I wanted to ask you how Maisy Perry is."

Red looked grim. "She's doing okay now that they pumped her stomach out. She was a

lucky lady that she got sick where she did. If she'd been at home then she probably wouldn't have made it. Having all the church ladies jump in like they did really made a difference."

"But she wasn't just *sick*, was she? I've never in my life seen someone get *that* sick, *that* fast. Was she ... poisoned?" She didn't want him to know that Elaine had been blabbing to her about it.

Red rubbed his eyes. "Yes, Mama, she was. Somehow her drink was poisoned with liquid nicotine. But I can't for the life of me think why someone would want to kill Maisy Perry. Did she upset someone with her horoscopes? I can't even ask her anything because she's still in bad shape. Seems like the whole town is going to hell."

"*Liquid* nicotine? So that means that it was in her drink?"

"That's right." Red glanced at his watch. "We'll have to catch up later, Mama. I've got to squeeze my workout in and then get back to work. Perkins and I have to get started in about an hour."

Myrtle raised her eyebrows questioningly when Red paused. "You coming?" he asked.

She groaned, threw her cup in the trash can and went in to face her doom.

Chapter Ten

Myrtle found, to her great surprise, that the workout wasn't as bad as she'd expected. The weights were set to her specifications, there were several people she knew in there (including Miles, who was already on the stair climbing machine and looked pleased to see her), and she felt like she had more energy at the end of the exercise. She made plans to return to Fit Life on Monday. But only, she told herself, because that would give her another chance to see Sherry and Simon.

Red, luckily hadn't seemed too upset by the fact that she was asking questions, and hopefully no one else was, either. Maybe Red was right. There was absolutely no reason for anyone to murder Maisy. She was fluffily innocuous and her horoscopes were a favorite feature in the *Bradley Bugle*. Besides, Willow had taken over writing the horoscopes for a whole week before Maisy was poisoned. If anyone was upset about a prediction, they had only Willow to blame.

But there were definitely reasons for someone to want to murder *Myrtle*. Most people just thought of her as a snoopy old lady. For someone who really had something to hide, though, they might consider her a threat. Erma's loud mouth at the visitation had broadcast that Myrtle knew exactly who the killer was. And then Sloan ran that big story about his octogenarian investigator. Myrtle locked her front door behind her as she went in—a rare daytime occurrence.

She opened the door back up again when there was a soft "meow" outside. Pasha, thought Myrtle. It was amazing how used she was getting to that cat. She'd really beefed up, too. She wasn't the scrawny creature she'd been a week ago. And she had all the tuna cans in the trap to thank for the fat grams.

"Hey, kitty," cooed Myrtle as she opened the front door. "How's Pasha today?"

Pasha darted in furtively and, to Myrtle's horror, appeared to have something in her mouth. "Pasha?"

Pasha turned and, seeing she had Myrtle's attention, made a great show of putting a chipmunk down on Myrtle's throw rug. To Myrtle's gaping horror, the chipmunk began hobbling around drunkenly. Pasha looked disapprovingly at Myrtle. It was clear that Myrtle was not doing what she was supposed to. She gave the chipmunk a swipe and looked up at Myrtle. Myrtle still stared openmouthed at the wounded creature. Finally, in disgust, Pasha lifted a paw and, swiftly brought it down again onto the chipmunk. She leaned over again and picked up the chipmunk by its neck and looked at Myrtle as if to say, "See? This is what you're supposed to do."

Myrtle opened the front door. Pasha shot her an icy glare and left with the chipmunk firmly in tow. Thankfully.

The chipmunk incident had completely destroyed her appetite. Which was a shame, since she'd been ravenous when she'd gotten back from exercising. And Elaine had given her a batch of her famous pimento cheese, too. Pity.

She looked at the clock. Her sidekick had left the gym before she had. He should be cleaned up and ready for a phone call by now, thought Myrtle.

"Okay," said Myrtle as soon as Miles picked up the phone. "I've overheard a little about Cullen and Simon and why they might want Jill dead. I have a pretty good idea about Sherry and Blanche's motives. And I know Georgia was upset with Jill over money. The problem is," said Myrtle, "that I don't have a good excuse to talk to Georgia. And I can't just go up to her house and knock on her door with no good reason to be nosy. If I start going around and having little afternoon teas with all the suspects, that would *really* worry the killer." Myrtle thought about the iced tea and wondered again if the killer was already on to her.

Miles straightened his steel-framed glasses. "Is Georgia a regular at Bo's Diner or anything? Does she have any kind of routine that you can interrupt?"

"I don't think so. I think she's trying to save money and doesn't really go out that much except to work and collect angels from garage sales."

"Well, can you go to her work?" asked Miles.

"That's no good. She works in a law office."

Miles blinked at this. "A law office. Looking like that?"

"I guess she has good typing and phone skills. Who knows? Maybe the lawyers were hard-up or something."

"Seems like you could just pop by her office for some made-up reason."

If I just walk through a lawyer's door it'll cost a hundred dollars." Myrtle sighed. Then she slapped her palm on Miles's end table. "I've got it! Since she collects ceramic angels, I'll invite her to come by and see my collection."

"You have a collection of ceramic angels?" Miles asked doubtfully.

"No, but I have a collection of gnomes. Aren't collectors interested in seeing other people's collections?"

"Not really," said Miles. "I think they're just interested in their own collections. You'd better try again."

"Or ... I could buy a few angels from the drugstore and then have a yard sale. Georgia said she spends her Saturday mornings combing yard sales for angels."

"Could you rummage up enough stuff to make up a yard sale? Your house seems pretty uncluttered."

Myrtle waved her hand dismissively. "I could dig up some old things to sell. Or Elaine can go in with me and put out some old baby clothes or something. She's been talking about having a yard sale for ages. And there's no time like the present."

"How 'present'?"

"This weekend, of course."

The yard sale merchandise was a little scarce, but there was definitely enough there to qualify it as a bona fide sale. Elaine had brought over a bunch of layette clothes, a baby exer-saucer, and assorted bottles, blankets, washcloths, and hooded towels. After thoroughly combing her house, Myrtle was able to come up with a few pots and pans (cooking wasn't Myrtle's favorite hobby, anyway), some old sheets, a few yellowing paperback books, and the angels she'd bought on the sale aisle of the drugstore.

Myrtle didn't have the patience to put stickers on everything, especially since she wasn't really interested in selling the stuff to begin with, and so grouped things together on blankets with signs indicating the price of everything on the blanket. It was a good thing she was a raging insomniac because a couple of what appeared to be professional yard sale shoppers rang her doorbell at five o'clock in the morning. Myrtle, who'd been up for two hours already, wasn't nearly as cross as she could have been. They took a few of the baby things, but when the couple turned their attention to the ceramic angels, Myrtle shooed them away. This done, she settled into a yard chair to wait for Georgia Simpson.

It didn't take long for Georgia to show up. She was in an aging pickup truck that under the best of circumstances was probably white. Myrtle noticed there were already clothes, books, and other odds and ends bundled in the back of the truck, so she knew she wasn't Georgia's first stop. Myrtle pushed herself out of her yard chair with some difficulty. "Hi Georgia!" she said.

Georgia barely gave her any sign of acknowledgement as she scanned the sale items. It was clear that Myrtle was faced with another yard sale pro. She took some of the baby clothes (the better ones, Myrtle noticed ... probably to resell them on the internet) and then gravitated inevitably to the ceramic angels, picking them up and cradling them in her hands.

"These almost look brand-new," she said in a reverent voice.

Imagine that. "They're in great condition, aren't they?" said Myrtle. "Georgia, I was wondering about what you said at the pancake breakfast ... "

"How much are you asking for them?" Georgia looked longingly at the little angels.

"Oh, I don't know," said Myrtle crossly. "Do you remember at the pancake breakfast when you were talking about Jill?"

Apparently, nothing else in the world existed but Georgia and the angels because once again she interrupted, "How much are you asking?" she murmured. "I just don't know if they're in my budget ... "

"Oh for heaven's sake! Just take the darned things," said Myrtle. At Georgia's startled expression, Myrtle continued in a sweeter voice, "I mean, feel free to accept them as a gift from me. I know how much you enjoy your angel collection and it would mean a great deal to me if you provide them with a good home."

Georgia was still looking at her with a perplexed expression. Myrtle said, "Sorry to jump down your throat like that, Georgia. It's been quite a week."

"I know what you mean, Miss Myrtle. *Every* week is like that for me. Well ... thanks. These little angels will fit right into my collection." She paused. "Was there something you were trying to ask me?"

Now that she had Georgia's full attention, Myrtle wasn't exactly sure how to proceed. "Uh. That's right, I was going to ask you about Jill's death." Georgia made a face and Myrtle hurried on, "You see, I think it's therapeutic for me to talk about it to people. It was just *so* traumatic coming across her body that way. Right in the middle of supper club, too!"

Georgia appeared somewhat discomfited. "I guess it would be a picture that would stick around in your head for a while. I wasn't with the supper club then, though. You know—I stayed behind. I fell asleep." She looked hard at Myrtle as if to search for any signs of disbelief.

Myrtle tried to direct the conversation back to the pancake breakfast. "I remember your saying that you were upset with Jill about something ... ." She trailed off the sentence in the hopes of eliciting information from Georgia, who was perilously close to being distracted by angels again.

Georgia snorted. "*Upset*? I was more than upset, Miss Myrtle. And you would be, too. Jill Caulfield robbed me. She robbed me just as much as if she'd taken a gun and held me up."

Myrtle waited and Georgia continued with an impatient sigh. "Jill and I went in together to buy lottery tickets at the gas station about six months ago. The deal was that if we won anything, we'd split it."

"And you got a winning ticket?" asked Myrtle. She hadn't heard anything about a lottery winner in Bradley, but then that wasn't usually the kind of news she spent much time following.

"Well, it was fifty thousand dollars! Not the big pot, but a lot of money, you know? She'd bought the tickets and held them, and then turned in the winning one herself. I guess she didn't want any lowlife relatives creeping out of the woodwork, so she didn't say anything about it to the newspaper."

"Didn't you confront her about it?" said Myrtle.

"I'll say I confronted her about it. Gave her a black eye, didn't I? Of course, everybody thought that Cullen gave it to her, and she let them think it because she liked people feeling sorry for her. Saint Jill." Georgia rolled her eyes.

"It seems like you could have found a lawyer at your office to get the money back for you," said Myrtle.

"Not really. It was her word against mine, right? It wasn't like we'd signed a contract with each other, and no one was around us when we decided to go in together to buy the tickets."

"So Jill had more money than I thought," said Myrtle, leaning forward onto her cane thoughtfully. "But she didn't do very much with it, did she?"

"Well, no," said Georgia in a sour voice, "She wouldn't, would she? Because of the Saint Jill thing. She wanted to work the two jobs and have everybody think she was God's gift. So she just sat on the money. But she was worth a lot more than people thought."

Was that enough money to kill for? Myrtle wondered about Jill's will. Was there a beneficiary whose life would improve with a quick infusion of cash?

"Besides," said Georgia, waving an angel in the air, "I wasn't the only person who had issues with Jill. Her own sister was fighting with her the night of her murder. So you can't tell me that there weren't others who saw through her phony-baloney stuff. Maybe Willow was trying to straighten her out." Georgia gave a vindictive toss of her head.

Myrtle was getting a little bored at the lack of new information. "Well, we all know that Willow was mad at Jill for not leaving Cullen. And she hated Cullen for being a bum and making Jill work to support them."

"I think it was more than that. Willow saw that Jill would rather complain about Cullen than divorce him. It was more like *Jill's* fault than Cullen's. Besides, Willow *hated* the way that Cullen treated Kojak, his dog. She'd get right up in his face and yell at him. Kept trying to kidnap the dog and take him to her house—then Cullen would show up and drag the animal back home. Cullen was just being spiteful because he didn't like Willow's meddling." Georgia shrugged her shoulders. She looked down at the angels she'd cradled in her arms. "Are you sure it's okay for me to take the angels, Miss Myrtle? I'm used to paying for things I want. *I'm* an honest person, anyway."

"I think the angels will be much happier at your house than mine, Georgia," said Myrtle.

As soon as Georgia left, Myrtle saw Red driving slowly down the street. He gave her a grim look. Rats, thought Myrtle. He must have seen Georgia. Well she had a perfectly legitimate reason for visiting. Myrtle smiled carelessly at Red and gave him a cheery wave. She could tell even from this distance that his face was a mottled red. She worried about his blood pressure sometimes.

Myrtle had actually tried to go to bed at a reasonable time, but the effort had proved a miserable failure. Warm milk, soothing bedtime routine, dull novel, the works. Nothing seemed to help. She decided to go on a walk, and glanced at the clock. Right before two a.m. Great ... now she was predictable, just like Erma was saying at the supper club.

She dressed and got her cane. The air outside was warm, despite the hour. She looked cautiously over at Erma's house but it was dark. She imagined adenoidal Erma snoring away and shuddered as she hustled past her house. She was very careful not to thump with her cane.

Miles's house was dark, too. It was probably his catch-up night. He seemed to go several days with no real sleep before catching up again during a couple of good nights. So this would just be a solo walk.

Her mind went back again to Jill's murder. Jill had been a puzzle to her—a mix of good and bad. Solving the case would be another feather in her cap, and a mini-blow to Red. She could find her *own* activities to do, thank you very much.

It was really a very quiet night, except for crickets chirping and some frogs calling to each other off in the distance. A lightening bug lit on Myrtle's arm, but she was so deep in her ruminations on the murder that she didn't even notice. She'd been surprised to discover that there were so many people who didn't like Jill. Sherry thought Jill was a candidate for World's Worst Neighbor. Blanche avoided Jill at all costs, whatever her reason was. Georgia seethed whenever Jill's name came up. Her own husband, Cullen, didn't seem to be that much of a fan. Her sister, Willow, was furious that Jill put up with Cullen in the first place. And Cullen said that Simon hadn't liked Jill either. Myrtle sighed. There was no shortage of suspects.

Myrtle later wondered why she'd never heard the car racing up behind her. She did hear, though, a sudden, raspy meow in the darkness as Myrtle felt a furry body brush against her leg. Myrtle turned abruptly, caught her toe in a gap in the sidewalk, dropped her cane, and went sprawling into a neighbor's yard ... just at the moment a car swung over the sidewalk, exactly where she'd been standing, before speeding off into the darkness.

Chapter Eleven

Myrtle didn't stay on the ground long. Injuries or no injuries, she was not going to be a sitting target for a killer. There was no sign of the cat and now she wondered if she'd imagined it. She felt around for her cane, grabbed it, got up, and hobbled to Miles's house. His initial exasperation at being awakened in the middle of the night was replaced with concern when he saw how shaken Myrtle was.

"Did you see the car?" asked Miles as he put a mug of hot tea in Myrtle's hands.

"No. I heard it, saw something rush off, but that was it. It didn't have its lights on."

"I guess not. This wasn't someone with safety on their mind." Miles put his teabag on his saucer.

"Who would want to kill you?" asked Miles. Actually, he could think of quite a few people. He'd qualify for that list from time to time. And Myrtle's son would be on it eighty-five percent of the time. "I mean, which of the *suspects*?"

Myrtle, fortunately, was not in an easily-insulted mood. "You know, I think this all goes back to blabbermouth Erma. She told half the town at the funeral home that I just needed a little bit of evidence and then I'd bag the killer. I'd imagine that most murderers would find that news a little discomfiting."

"Okay, you say half the town, but really, who was there? I can't remember much except that Erma was making a fool of herself as usual."

"Out of our favorite suspects? Georgia was there," Myrtle ignored the flush that crept up Miles's face. "Sherry was there. Cullen was somewhere around there, but I don't know what kind of condition he was in. Sherry could have told Cullen. Willow was there, although she seemed more upset about Erma's graphic depiction of the crime scene. Simon and Libba were still greeting visitors, but Cullen could have told them about it later. So ... basically everyone was there."

"And you weren't denying Erma's blathering."

"Well no. She was being too darned interesting for once. I wanted to see where she was going with it all."

Miles sighed. "Actually, it doesn't really matter who was there or not. It was on the front page of the local rag, remember? Either someone thinks you're getting too close to the truth, or they're worried you're going to. Your nosiness may not seem so harmless anymore. Last time you were nosy, you helped solve a murder. Now you probably seem more like a crime fighter than a snoopy old lady."

Miles hid a smile at the idea of a strident Myrtle in storm trooper gear out annihilating evil. "So, actually, you don't really know anything. You just told Erma that you did because you were irritated with her. And she blabbed this lie to half the town."

Myrtle was miffed. "I certainly *do* know a few things. During the course of my investigation I've found out lots of interesting tidbits."

Miles raised his eyebrows.

"Well first of all, I know that *someone* knew I take little middle of the night walks. They were familiar enough with my habit to wait for me to come out and then try to run me down."

Miles nodded. "So who would know about that?"

Myrtle snorted. "Just about anybody. Erma bellowed it out during the supper club for anyone to hear. Remember? She was making fun of the way I was thumping with my cane."

"Right. And there were a lot of people standing around, although I can't really remember who was that close."

"*Everyone* was that close. No offence, Miles, but we were all standing at very close quarters."

Myrtle stirred her tea while she thought. "I also know Blanche Clark was afraid of Jill, but I really don't know why." She paused. "But I *think* it might have something to do with Jill's snooping. Maybe Jill was blackmailing Blanche, or maybe Blanche was just worried that Jill *could* blackmail her. Or Blanche is just worried that people would talk."

"I don't really understand," said Miles, "why, if Jill really *did* have some information on Blanche, why Blanche would really care. You mentioned that Jill was snooping in your medicine cabinet, so I'm guessing she might have snooped in Blanche's too. I mean, if she has some sort of a medical problem or some kind of an addiction, won't people just understand that she needs help?"

"People .... .you mean like people where you moved from? City people? Urban people? *Atlanta* people?" Myrtle snorted inelegantly. "Sure, *those* type of people would bring Blanche a casserole, tell her about their Uncle Edwin's pill problem, and give her the number of the nearest chichi rehab facility. Then they'll promptly forget the incident ever happened and descend back into the chaos of their daily lives."

"But not Bradley people?"

"Bradley people know that there's not really any other news to talk about. They will absolutely run Blanche's pill problem into the ground by gabbing about it all the time. They'll bless her heart, then yak and yak and yak about it. On her deathbed, she'll still be Poor-Blanche-Who-Did-Drugs. Remember Katy Johnson? No, you wouldn't because she ran away from Bradley before you got here. But if you ask anybody about Katy, will they say that she was sweet as homemade pie? Will they mention that she organized the toy drive for the underprivileged children? No, it'll all be "Katy-Who-Lost-Her-Whole-Bathing-Suit-in-that-Water-Skiing-Contest."

"And you said that Georgia was upset with Jill," Miles took off his glasses and polished them.

"*Upset* doesn't even really cover it. I think *spitting mad* is more the term. Georgia thinks Jill cheated her out of her share of a lottery win."

"How did your visit with Georgia go?" asked Miles in a careless voice.

"I'd have taken you with me," said Myrtle carefully, "if I hadn't thought you'd turn my interrogation into a social visit."

Myrtle added hurriedly, "So, yes, Georgia is a natural suspect. And there's also Jill's neighbor Sherry. Sherry knows Erma Sherman and she *still* claims that Jill was a worse neighbor than Erma is. So now we know that Sherry is a drama queen. Because *no one* is a worse neighbor than Erma."

"Why did Sherry think that Jill was so awful?"

Myrtle snorted. "Some ridiculous reason like 'Jill was too perfect' or something like that. I can only *dream* of having a neighbor who is so meticulous about her yard that it's annoying. Oh, and Jill's Christmas lights and music bugs her. I think she might even have been having an affair with Cullen just to get back at Jill."

"Wait. Stop right there. The bad neighbor stuff isn't such a big deal, but you didn't tell me that Sherry and Cullen are having an affair."

"That's right. It's been going on for a while, apparently. That's what Simon alluded to, anyway. He was accusing Cullen of murdering Jill so that he could marry Sherry. And while we're mentioning Simon, he's never been a big fan of Jill's either. I think he's always thought Jill wasn't good enough for his brother."

Miles snorted. "That's a good one. Like *Cullen* is actually good enough for anyone."

"Yes, but I taught those boys. The family was a good one and well-respected at the time. The father had plenty of money and they were one of the wealthier families in Bradley. So it's definitely possible that Simon would have looked down on Jill, who was from a working class family."

"And killed her after so many years?" Miles looked doubtful. "Did anyone else want to get rid of Jill?"

Myrtle thought. "Willow. I've heard several accounts now—one from you—about how Willow and Jill were arguing right before Jill was murdered. And then they fought with each other at your party. It always seemed to be over Jill's marriage. Willow wanted Jill to leave Cullen."

"That's sort of a leap to murdering your sister, though, isn't it?" asked Miles. "You won't leave this good-for-nothing lout. So I'm going to *kill* you?"

Myrtle shrugged. "Maybe she'd just had enough of her family, period. Lord knows I feel that way about Red sometimes."

"So Blanche, Georgia, Sherry, Simon, Cullen, and Willow had issues with Jill Caulfield. But everyone else thought she was this salt-of-the-earth do-gooder," said Miles. "And whoever Jill's killer is must be someone we know. Someone we think of as a friend, someone we went to supper club with. But this someone is perfectly happy to try to mow you down with their car. Shouldn't we be calling the police or something?"

Myrtle looked away from Miles. "Do we have to? I mean, really, what good is it going to do? I'm just going to get a lecture from Red about wandering around in the middle of the night again. And he'll point out that I *did* fall down, which had nothing to do with the murderer and everything to do with Pasha. Poor cat. Did a good deed for me and then took off again into the night."

"He *might* be able to find out who did it. He could do a quick check of the neighbors' cars and see if one's missing."

"The car has probably quietly coasted back into its driveway by now. And half the houses in question have garages so you can't see what's parked inside. Plus, I have no description of the car. I can't describe the driver or the sound of the motor. It's been dry as a bone outside so there won't be any tire tracks. The car didn't hit anything, so there won't be chipped paint or anything. Let's just leave it alone."

Myrtle suddenly remembered the poisoned iced tea. So this made a *second* attempt on her life. She opened her mouth to say something to Miles about it, then snapped it shut again. Best not to tell Miles about it because he really *would* talk to Red. And it's not like Myrtle had any real evidence of foul play.

"And be *careful*," said Miles.

"Yes. Very careful," said Myrtle. "As I continue my investigations."

Miles looked as though his head hurt.

"I'm *going* to be careful, Miles. But I'm going to have the biggest story of my journalism career at the same time. I just need to do some digging. And I know things are going to get even harder. Red wasn't happy about finding me walking around at night by myself. And now every time I open my front door I see him somewhere close by. He's driving me crazy."

"He is?" asked Miles. "So the tables are turned, then?"

Myrtle ignored him. "He's sticking to me like a leech. He's everywhere. He's like God." Myrtle sounded completely deflated.

"Things *must* be bad if you're attributing God-like properties to Red," said Miles with concern.

"Doesn't he have a case to solve or something? I'm not going to be able to do any questioning this way at all. And I really do need to talk to Blanche Clark."

"Why not have Blanche come to you?" suggested Miles.

"Come again?"

"You could pretend you're temporarily home-bound with some sort of illness or something. Doesn't Blanche work on that church committee?"

"Actually, I think Blanche and Tippy *are* that church committee. Miles, you're a genius."

"Thanks," said Miles modestly.

The next morning, Myrtle set the Bereavement and Illness committee into motion. Myrtle smiled when the doorbell rang. That should be Blanche now, food in tow. This suspect interview couldn't possibly end badly; even if Myrtle didn't get any information at all, she'd at least end up with a delicious casserole. Her only worry, as she thumped across the living room with her cane, was that someone else from the church was subbing for Blanche. What if it was Prissy Daniels at the door instead? Myrtle shuddered.

It was Blanche. Myrtle sighed with relief. She was wearing black slacks and a silky green blouse and a beautiful scarf held in place with a pin. Myrtle, who had always wanted to be able to carry off wearing a scarf, eyed it jealously. Blanche sure looked a lot jauntier since Jill's murder.

Blanche walked right into Myrtle's kitchen and put the casserole in the fridge, talking as she did about the cooking instructions. "How are you feeling?" she asked with concern.

Myrtle, who had almost forgotten she was supposed to be sick, said, "Oh, I'm hanging in there, Blanche. Just barely, of course." She coughed weakly. She couldn't for the life of her remember what illness she'd concocted. Was she supposed to have an upset stomach? Strep? A bad cold? She searched the dark recesses of her mind. No, she decided, it was flu. Which explained why Blanche was keeping a healthy distance from her.

Blanche smiled at Myrtle, but preserved her personal space. "Did the doctor say when you might be feeling better?"

Myrtle frowned. The conversation was not supposed to be centered around her health, lack of it or otherwise. "I didn't go in. He ... uh ... diagnosed me on the phone. I don't think he wanted me to come in and spread germs around his waiting room."

This was obviously the wrong thing to say. Blanche increased the distance between them and eased toward the door. "Well, I hope you're feeling better soon, Myrtle."

Myrtle said hastily, "Oh, I'm sure I'll be better soon. The doctor prescribed an anti-viral, you see." It wouldn't do to have Blanche see her traipsing around later that day. She'd have to remember to be careful. Obviously she'd have to pass on going to the gym today. Shoot.

"It's been such an awful week," Myrtle continued. "What with poor Jill's murder and then my getting sick ... it's been one thing after another." She saw Blanche's eyes narrow. Myrtle didn't want to scare Blanche off. She started prattling.

"I just couldn't believe it when we saw Jill on the floor like that. What a shock! Who could have done such a thing, Blanche? I live here all by myself, you know, and I am just scared to death that someone's going to come here and try to smother me with my own pillow or something." Myrtle wrung her hands. She'd never actually seen anyone wring their hands or done it herself. But in the spur of the moment, it seemed like a good thing to do.

Blanche's voice was gentle. "I don't think you have anything to worry about, Myrtle. Red is right across the street from you: you can't be any safer than that! The police chief himself. Besides, Jill was probably killed over something personal. You don't have anyone that mad at you."

Myrtle made a face. "Red probably qualifies as that mad, sometimes. But he won't take a whack at me anytime soon." She paused. "You know, it was a funny thing about Jill. She did a really bang-up job with cleaning. The whole place shone. But she was so very interested in my medicine cabinet."

Blanche looked swiftly up at her.

"Not that there was anything in there but Q-tips and witch hazel. But, I was wondering if she'd found something more interesting in yours?"

Blanche abruptly took a seat on Myrtle's sofa. "You haven't told anyone? Not even Red?"

"Of course not!" She wouldn't mention Miles. "But I don't understand why you won't go to the police over it. They're bound to find out. And you were a victim."

Blanche took a deep breath and let go of Myrtle's arm. "I was in a car accident a while ago—before I moved here. My back was a mess and the recovery was really painful, so the doctor prescribed me painkillers. But once you start taking painkillers, it's hard to get off of them. My doctor stopped prescribing them for me so I started getting them from a dealer."

"But Jill wouldn't have known if you had a current prescription or not."

"She knew," said Blanche bitterly. "Oxycodone isn't a long-term prescription for people these days. Not for people who aren't in a great deal of pain. No, Jill knew *exactly* what was going on and exactly what kind of a barrel she had me over."

"She blackmailed you," said Myrtle.

"Yes." Blanche studied a spot on the wall over Myrtle's head.

"Would it have mattered so much?" asked Myrtle. "People would have found out that you had an addiction—but they'd have forgotten about it eventually."

Blanche gave a short laugh. "You, more than anybody, Myrtle, know that's not true. You've lived in Bradley long enough to know that people here *never* forget. I'd never be able to continue doing all the things I'm doing now. All the committees I'm on? I'd probably be given the cold shoulder at most of the clubs I'm in."

The thought made Blanche look sicker than Myrtle was supposed to be.

Myrtle said, "You're not the first person to be addicted to prescription drugs, you know. Don't be too hard on yourself. There are plenty of places to get help."

Blanche gave her a small smile. "Thanks, Myrtle."

"I'm surprised," said Myrtle in a musing voice, "considering the street value of the drugs Jill discovered, that she didn't just swipe them and resell them on the street."

"She probably thought about it," said Blanche. "But it would be a lot riskier than blackmail. There would have been more of a chance of discovery."

"So you paid Jill to keep it quiet?"

Blanche looked tired. "I did. I felt like I had to. And then I fired her. I couldn't bear having her around me anymore." She said the words like they were sour on her tongue.

Abruptly, Blanche lurched to her feet and walked to the door. "I've got to go now, Myrtle. Please ... you will keep this quiet, won't you?"

Myrtle said warmly, "Of course I will."

Blanche smiled weakly at Myrtle, then pulled open the front door. And shrieked.

Pasha stood in the doorway holding a live snake. Myrtle grabbed her cane from the coat rack by the door and shook it at the cat as Blanche shrank backwards in alarm, whether at the snake, the cat, or the cane-brandishing Myrtle she wasn't sure. "Shoo! Shoo, Pasha!"

Pasha looked resentfully at her and carried her prey off to the side of the house. Myrtle turned and squeezed Blanche's arm apologetically. "Pasha thinks I need hunting lessons," Myrtle said in a feeble voice.

Blanche's laugh bordered on the hysterical. "It's fine, Myrtle. As long as it's gone. I ... um ... hope you feel better." She looked doubtfully at Myrtle, still holding her cane with a robust stance.

"Blanche," said Myrtle, "I think I feel better already."

Chapter Twelve

Myrtle and Miles sat next to each other in padded rocking chairs on Myrtle's front porch while Myrtle gave Miles the lowdown on Blanche's visit.

"Okay," said Myrtle. "That worked. But I don't think I can trick anyone else into coming by to visit. I'm going to have to go out and about—go by Fit Life, nose around and listen for some scuttlebutt. I'm starting to worry that Red and the state police are getting ahead of me in the investigation. After all, *they* get all the forensic information and all that stuff. I'd like to send them off on a wild goose chase. Something just to get them off the scent. Maybe it'll give them something else to think about while I solve the case."

"And *why* are you solving cases again? I keep forgetting," said Miles in a weary voice.

"Right *now* why am I doing it? Because Red keeps trying to mess in my business. So let's let him see how it feels!" said Myrtle, vigorously rocking the rocking chair.

"What kind of a red herring are you sending them off on?" asked Miles.

"I need to have Red think they're finding out something I don't want them to know. Otherwise, they won't do a thing about it. Maybe I could imprudently leave my notebook behind, or my voice recorder. Or I could leave a file up on my computer. Or ... "

"Or you could just let them overhear us talking," breathed Miles under his breath. "Because I just saw Red walking up from the side. I think he's lurking behind the bushes next to the porch now."

"Like I was saying," said Myrtle in a louder voice, "I just couldn't believe what Jill had found out. I never would have known it except I heard her talking on her cell phone to Cullen that day she was cleaning my house. I couldn't figure out at *first* who she was talking about," said Myrtle, "but then I realized." She took a deep breath and smiled as she was struck by what seemed like a brilliant idea. "Erma Sherman!"

Miles blinked at Myrtle from behind his glasses. Then he smiled admiringly at her, "What did Jill have on Erma?"

"Well apparently, Jill has been doing some cleaning for Erma and poking around in Erma's business, like she liked to do. And she discovered a really *horrible* medical problem. It seemed that Erma had this awful condition. Something *catching*, too. Something Erma wouldn't want anyone to know about because it would mean people would actually *avoid* her."

"Imagine that," said Miles dryly. "People avoiding Erma. Such a notion."

"Um, anyway, Miles, why don't we go inside for a little while. This heat is really making me parched and I could use a glass of iced tea."

Miles followed Myrtle obediently inside then watched as she peered through a curtain. "There he goes!" said Myrtle triumphantly and Red hurried across the side of Myrtle's yard. "He's feeling lucky that he happened to be in the right place in the right time."

"Think he'll march over and interview Erma?"

"I think he'll grab Lieutenant Perkins first, and maybe some surgical masks to keep the germs away," said Myrtle. She pushed aside the white curtains and shoved the window up. "I can usually hear his car engine a mile away. Especially with the window open."

"I think this sounds like a good time for me to go back home and have some lunch," said Miles. "What are you planning on doing, Miss Marple? Grilling suspects? Dusting for fingerprints? Using your little gray cells?"

"Poirot had the little gray cells," said Myrtle with a sniff. "No, I'm planning on giving

my brain a short rest. I'm going to watch *Tomorrow's Promise*. That's a soap opera, Miles. And I *might* even take a little nap. After some rejuvenation, I'm sure I can piece together all the clues."

At the exciting conclusion of *Tomorrow's Promise*, there was a familiar pounding at Myrtle's front door. She groaned. It had to be Erma. Myrtle knew that pummeling anywhere. Myrtle picked up her cane and moved quietly to the front door, peeping out the window. It was Erma, her rat-like face now peering directly *into* the window Myrtle was looking out of. Myrtle jumped half out of her skin.

She'd been spotted. Now there was nothing else to do but open the door. Thinking fast, Myrtle also grabbed her pocketbook from the wooden coat rack near the door. If she said she was on her way out, she could expedite this unexpected visit. And could keep Erma on the front porch where she wouldn't get too cozy.

"Myrtle," shrilled Erma. "I had the weirdest visit from your boy. And that other policeman."

"Detective Lieutenant Perkins, you mean?" asked Myrtle. She reached behind her to turn the ceiling fan on in the hopes of cooling off her temper, and then plopped wearily into a rocking chair. Erma sat down abruptly, and then rocked forward, wagging her finger at Myrtle.

"Red came quite unexpectedly. He and that Polkens asked all these peculiar questions. Do you know anything about why they did that?" Erma's narrow eyes managed to squint even more.

"I never get *any* information from Red about his investigations," said Myrtle quite truthfully. "Erma, I was on my way out the door ... "

"It was almost like they were working on a tip that *I* had employed Jill. And that I knew something about the murder. I don't know a thing about it. But I did tell them all about my cyst. They seemed really interested in it. Why wouldn't they be? It's such an unusual problem; my doctor said he'd never seen anything like it. At first I thought it was some weird pimple, but then it grew to the size of a quarter. The doctor was puzzled: was it an ingrown hair? A calcium deposit? A fatty tumor? He lanced the cyst and then ... "

At that moment a miracle occurred. Or so it seemed to Myrtle. Pasha appeared from the side of the house. She loped purposefully up the stairs and inserted herself directly in front of Erma—the antithesis of normal feral cats' behavior with strangers. It assessed Erma, loathed her on sight, and began a low, menacing growl from way in the back of its throat.

Erma's transformation was astonishing. Her eyes, so filled with eagerness with recounting the story, widened so you could see the whites on all sides. Her mouth became a giant O and she pushed backwards with her feet until the rocker's legs scraped the paint on the front of Myrtle's house. "Get it *away*," she bellowed.

Myrtle was too startled by Erma's reaction and the cat's hatred to do anything at first. Pasha's fur stood straight up on end and it arched its back, hissing.

Erma started wheezing and her eyes watered. "Allergic!" she said hoarsely. Myrtle unenthusiastically shooed the cat, but it wouldn't budge. The best of all possible outcomes happened when Erma finally bolted up from her chair and hurried off the porch, sneezing. She gave Myrtle a hurried, dismissive wave as she staggered off to her house, slamming the door behind her with a bang.

Myrtle looked at the cat, now sitting on the rocker and licking its fur with satisfaction. "Pasha," said Myrtle thoughtfully. "You may be my new best friend."

Unfortunately for Myrtle's investigation, her brain rejuvenation was wasted on blogging and her next helpful hints column. Myrtle did manage to justify this to herself, though. After all, if Sloan fired her because she wasn't meeting her deadlines, then she wasn't going to have her big story as an investigative reporter for the *Bradley Bugle*.

She'd actually gotten a fair number of tips in her email this week. Most of them seemed to deal with stain removal. Myrtle took this to mean that the people of Bradley, North Carolina, were a clumsy lot who drank lots of red wine, chewed bubble gum, and marked themselves up with ball point pens. Still, it was good to know that adding a couple of Alka-Seltzer tablets to the bottom of a glass vase removes stains. Next time she got flowers, she'd have to remember that. She wondered if Red would send her flowers after she solved his case for him.

A nine o'clock knock on her door surprised Myrtle. It was starting to be like Grand Central Station at her house. Nine o'clock was late for visitors, but it was still a little light outside, since it was summer. She peeked out the side window in case it was Erma. Or in case it was someone who didn't need to see her in her nightgown and robe. Willow Pearce stood on her front porch and gave her a small smile and lifted up a casserole for her to see.

Myrtle opened the door. "Willow! You brought me a present?"

Willow smiled again. She was looking a little better than she had in the days following Jill's murder. "Blanche and Tippy told me you'd been under the weather. I cooked you up a casserole with my own herbs and produce from my garden." She walked in, bearing a foil casserole container that she held with tie-dye oven mitts.

"Just set it down on the counter, won't you? And sit down and visit for a few minutes. I've been thinking about you lately," said Myrtle. This was more than she'd hoped for, to actually have a chance to talk to Willow without chasing her down. She felt like she'd come up with enough trumped-up reasons for interviewing suspects with this case.

Willow sat down in Myrtle's high-backed armchair and managed to look pleased with herself as well as ill at ease. Or maybe it was just all that fiber Willow ate that made her look uncomfortable. Myrtle liked vegetables as much as the next person, but she sure wouldn't want a one-hundred percent vegetable diet.

Myrtle knit her brows. There was something about Willow that she needed to remember. She couldn't put her finger on what it was.

Willow, fortunately, hadn't seemed to notice that she was the focus of Myrtle's frowning perusal. She was talking about the growing season this year and the problems the drought had caused.

Myrtle broke in. "You grow a lot of vegetables, don't you? But you don't have any hens or anything like that, do you? I remember when I was a girl that we were always self-sufficient because my parents grew their own food. Is that why you like gardening so much, Willow?"

Willow shook her head, long white hair shimmying around her shoulders. "No, I don't care so much about being self-sufficient. For me, it's to get fresh vegetables. *Organically grown* fresh vegetables."

"Because you're a vegetarian. Is that right?" Myrtle caught her breath as realization washed over her. Why would Willow have been back at Jill's the next day getting barbeque? She wouldn't— not for herself. She must have been back to get her casserole dish … the one she swore she hadn't dropped off the night of the party.

Willow was unaware of Myrtle's horror. "That's right. Did we talk about that some time?" She looked curiously at Myrtle.

"Elaine mentioned it to me at the luncheon. You know, the United Methodist Women luncheon. Elaine commented because you'd brought your own dish to the buffet."

Willow gave a short laugh. "The ladies call those green beans vegetarian. But they're cooked in animal fat! What kind of vegetarian would eat that? So of course I bring my own food to their luncheons."

Myrtle realized that Willow would, of course, have brought her own food to Jill's house. Otherwise, there would have been nothing there for her to eat. Jill would have served barbeque and the baked beans were pork and beans. And—those tie dyed oven mitts that Willow was holding looked exactly like what she should have had in her kitchen. The rooster potholders she'd seen the night of the supper club had looked so out of place. They must have been Myrtle's—taken from Jill's house. Did Willow hold the frying pan up with them as she hit Jill with the fatal blow?

Willow's gray-blue eyes were piercing Myrtle. "Are you okay, Miss Myrtle? You look ... tired."

"Yes," said Myrtle quickly. "I *am* tired, Willow. Why don't we visit another time? Thanks for the casserole, though. I'll look forward to eating it tomorrow."

"Or maybe for a midnight snack?" Willow smiled. "I know you're up a lot at night. Probably why you're so tired now."

Myrtle shivered. Yes, Willow knew she was an insomniac. She'd been the one to try and mow her down. She gripped her cane and struggled to her feet.

"You don't have to show me out," said Willow quickly. "I know the way." She left just as fast as she'd arrived.

Myrtle wasted no time. She stood up and walked stiffly over to the wall phone in the kitchen. "Red?" she said. "Listen. You've got to come over. I need to talk to you." Red interrupted her and she raised her voice. "I've figured out ... "

At that moment, the phone was punched out of her hand. Myrtle spun around and saw Willow's face just inches from her own. "I let myself back in, too," she gritted, her face barely recognizable and not at all like the mild-mannered herbalist she usually was. "I thought you looked like you were up to something."

Chapter Thirteen

Myrtle reached behind her for something, anything, as Willow gripped her shoulders and shook her back and forth in anger. "I kept trying to get rid of you. Nosy busybody," Willow said. She put her hands around Myrtle's throat right when Myrtle finally curled her fingers around the foil container. With one, desperate gesture, Myrtle pushed the container of vegetable casserole in Willow's face.

Willow howled like a hurt dog and spat furiously to get the casserole out of her mouth. God knows what poison she's put in there, thought Myrtle as she anxiously hobbled to the door, her cane nowhere near her. She'd just reached the door when Willow's hand jerked back on her shoulder and Myrtle stumbled backwards, just as Red pushed through Myrtle's front door. With a wild cry, Willow launched herself at Red.

Red strong-armed Willow's hands behind her back and struggled to put the cuffs on as Willow twisted violently from side to side. "I never thought I'd say this," said Red through gritted teeth, "but I'm glad you had your door unlocked, Mama."

Myrtle rubbed her neck where Willow's hands had gripped. "An unlocked door was great when *you* were on my doorstep. But clearly I should have locked the door back right after Willow left."

Willow had given up her fight and stood, slumped, as Red read her rights to her and walked her out the door and across the street to his police car parked in his driveway. Myrtle watched through the window as Red talked on his phone and Willow sat in the back of the police car.

The first call Red made must have been to Miles because he was at her door a few minutes later, looking sleepy and wearing a very un-Miles-like sweat suit. "Come on in," said Myrtle. "I guess Red must have called you." She walked towards the kitchen, "I'll make us some coffee." She stopped cold at her kitchen door when she saw the disaster her kitchen was. There was food all over the table, chairs and floor, tracked all the way into her living room. One of the chairs was turned over. Myrtle shivered.

Miles looked over her shoulder and said, "I don't know what happened here, Myrtle, but I think *I* should be the one making the coffee. Do I need to clean all the mess up first?"

Myrtle sat down on her sofa and rubbed her eyes. "No, better not. It's probably poisoned and might need to be used as evidence." A wave of exhaustion hit her.

"Well frankly, Myrtle, your place sounds like a lousy place for a coffee break right now. Let's walk on over to my house." Miles adopted a coaxing tone and Myrtle collected her cane and obediently followed him out the door. Red nodded at them as they passed. He was still on his phone as they left.

It wasn't long before Lieutenant Perkins and Red were at Miles's house drinking coffee along with Myrtle. Perkins settled his tall, wiry frame on Miles's leather chair.

"This is starting to be a familiar scene," remarked Perkins in a dry voice. "Didn't we do this after the last Bradley murder case wrapped up?"

"I think it was wine, then," said Myrtle, looking at Miles with reproach.

Miles rolled his eyes and walked to his kitchen.

"What I actually meant," said Perkins in his polite, measured way, "is that we're replaying a particular scene. And it's not a healthy one."

Red jumped in. "You're going to get yourself killed, Mama. You're playing a very dangerous game. You know that I'm supposed to be the detective around here."

"I can't help it if I figure out the mystery before you do," said Myrtle coldly. "Besides, I had nothing to do with what happened at my house. I solved the case *while* Willow was there. It wasn't as if I lured her to my house." She hesitated for a minute. "I don't know if you need any additional charges against Willow, but I think this is the third time she's tried to kill me. Or maybe the fourth." At the loud exclamations of Red and Perkins, she hurried on, "Well, I think she probably intended to poison me instead of Maisy at the United Methodist Women luncheon. It was *my* iced tea. Then she tried to run me down in her car." She waved her hands impatiently. "I didn't know it was her at the time!"

"You could have *told* us," said Perkins, hushing the spluttering Red. "If you'd told us there'd been an attempt on your life then maybe we could have figured out who was behind it."

"But there wouldn't have been any evidence. And I didn't see anything."

"What," asked Red in a carefully modulated voice, "were the third and fourth times?"

"There's a vegetable casserole in my kitchen. Actually, it's all over my kitchen. I'm pretty sure that it's poisoned, judging from Willow's reaction when some of it got in her mouth. And the fourth time would have been this." And Myrtle pulled on the collar of her robe to show the angry marks around her neck where Willow had squeezed her hands.

"What I don't really understand," said Lieutenant Perkins slowly, "is why she was so determined to get rid of you. It's not like you knew anything." He raised his eyebrows questioningly at Myrtle and looked at her searchingly with his steady, gray eyes. "Is it? *Did* you know something?"

Myrtle frowned indignantly at Perkins. "If I'd known anything, I certainly wouldn't have let Willow into my house at nine o'clock at night. No, I think she just knew I was on the *verge* of knowing something. And she knew, of course, that I was nosing around. Erma Sherman was blabbing about how I was about to solve the case and Willow was right there. And then Sloan ran that piece in the paper about his octogenarian investigative reporter who was hot on the scent. I'm sure that didn't exactly help."

"I'll have to have a little talk with Sloan," said Red. Miles came back in with a couple of wine glasses and a bottle of wine. He gave Myrtle a sympathetic look. Having Red cramp her style at the newspaper was not going to go over well.

"Let's talk about this detective work," said Perkins, with a silencing look at Red. "What exactly did you find out? You say you didn't know anything until tonight?"

Myrtle sighed. "Well, I had all the pieces in front of me, but I didn't put it together until Willow came over. Which is unfortunate. I guess she could tell that I'd had some sort of a revelation. After all, she'd been expecting one all along." She remembered Willow's strangely piercing eyes.

"It was the vegetable casserole, you see. And we were talking about her organic vegetable and herb garden. She's this healthy-living hippy. I remembered she brought her own food to the United Methodist Women luncheon because she didn't want any vegetables that were cooked in chicken broth or pork. But then I remembered how she told me she was getting barbeque the day after Jill was killed."

"It didn't make any sense," said Myrtle. "It made a lot more sense that she went back there to get her casserole dish. The dish she said she *never took there*. Because if she'd taken her own food to Jill's like she usually did, it would have placed her on the scene of the crime. And she didn't want to risk that."

"Plus," said Myrtle, "once I thought about her whole healthy living credo, I realized that it was very odd that she would have been buying cigarettes at the store. When Elaine told me that, I just chalked it up to Willow being unpredictable. Then I remembered how toxic nicotine in liquid form actually is. And

Willow, as a former nurse, would have known that. Red, didn't you tell me that Maisy was poisoned by nicotine?"

Perkins and Red nodded. "But why," asked Perkins, "wouldn't Willow just have used something from her garden? She probably has all sorts of dangerous plants in her back yard."

"It would have pointed everybody in her direction, wouldn't it? She's the herb expert. No, it had to be something that she ordinarily wouldn't have been associated with. Willow had already decided I knew who did it, because of Erma and Sloan. And tonight she could tell that I'd finished adding things up. She was going to have to finish me off before I pegged her as the killer."

"What I don't understand," said Red, "is why she murdered her sister at all. Sure, they had the odd argument, but nothing to commit murder over."

"All of the arguments had a common theme," pointed out Myrtle. "Cullen. Willow thought Jill needed to leave him. She was sure that Cullen was abusing her sister, not to mention making her work two jobs while he did nothing."

Perkins nodded. "So you think she planned on killing Cullen that night."

"I don't think she *planned* to do anything. I think she went over to Jill's house to leave a vegetarian dish there that she could eat."

"So," said Myrtle, "she entered the house. Jill and Cullen were there. They were probably arguing. Jill wasn't happy that Cullen didn't pick up the phone when she only wanted him to stir the barbeque and check on the food. Maybe Jill discovered that Cullen was having an affair with Sherry ... Sherry left Miles's house early and Jill could have seen Cullen leaving Sherry's house when she was on her way home. They argued. We know Cullen was drunk and in a bad temper. It could have gotten violent."

"But," said Red, "everyone said that Cullen was passed out in the back of the house when they came over."

"True. He probably passed out at some point during the argument with Jill. Or maybe Jill clobbered *him* for a change. Either way, Willow heard a fight. And she decided, on the spur of the moment, to defend her sister. She picked up the cast iron skillet with my cute rooster oven mitts," noted Myrtle with some lingering irritation, "and swung as soon as the kitchen door opened."

"But it wasn't Cullen," said Red.

"No. And Willow must have been horrified at her mistake. But she had to act fast. She made sure that Cullen hadn't seen or heard anything. Then she realized she couldn't be gone too long from the party, so she hurried back to Miles's house."

Miles said thoughtfully, "In sort of a wildly colored outfit."

"But maybe it wasn't wildly colored," said Myrtle. "Maybe it had blood splattered on it. With those print dresses she wears, it can be hard to tell."

"And she left pretty abruptly," noted Miles.

"She used the drink tray spilling as an excuse to go change. She was going to be the hostess at the next house. She needed to change her clothes and make sure no one suspected anything," said Myrtle. She paused. "I actually noticed my rooster oven mitts when I was in her kitchen looking for iced tea. They looked out of place to me in her new age kitchen, but I never dreamed they actually *were* mine. But it clicked into place when I saw the mitts she wore when she brought me the casserole today. They were these 60s-inspired tie dye looking things. Not kitschy roosters."

"And she's been trying to cover it all up since then," said Perkins. "It's a wonder she didn't try to pin it all on Cullen."

"She did!" said Myrtle. "But of course no one took her really seriously. We all knew she couldn't stand him. But Cullen *was* passed out, after all. He didn't seem to be faking it. Which was actually a fairly good alibi."

Red stood up. "I'd better run—I need to go get Willow processed through the system." He stooped and gave Myrtle an unexpected kiss on the cheek. "Good job, Mama."

Myrtle beamed. "And good job to you for wrestling that homicidal maniac."

"You were actually doing all right on your own. That was quick thinking with slinging the poisoned casserole." Red turned to Miles. "Thanks again for providing us with a place to unwind. And the coffee."

Lieutenant Perkins followed Red out the door, talking with him about the case as they went. Miles, who had been looking uncomfortably underdressed in his sweat suit, cleared his throat and said, "You know, Myrtle, I think I'm ready to hit the sack. Actually, I was already in bed-mode when Red called."

"Sorry," said Myrtle. She looked around for a clock and saw that it was eleven o'clock. "I guess time flies during life and death struggles." She sighed. "I guess half the town will be out milling in the street to see all the action."

They peeked out the door with caution and saw a deserted street. "Where are all the spectators?" demanded Myrtle. "Doesn't anyone realize what was going on here?"

"Apparently not," said Miles. "But think about it ... .there were no sirens or blue lights. Red just ran across the street and then walked back across with Willow to put her in the car. And Lieutenant Perkins probably drove in quietly. There's no murder so there's not a huge forensics team taking pictures or roping the place off. There are probably just a couple of people over there collecting evidence to use against Willow."

"I guess I'll need to keep out of their way," said Myrtle. "Which won't be hard since I'm going directly to bed. Today is finally catching up with me."

Miles walked her home and inside her house. The two officers inside just motioned which area to keep away from and Myrtle headed off to bed. "Just lock the door behind you," said Myrtle. "Although I guess it's not so dangerous anymore."

Chapter Fourteen

It was still very early in the day, particularly since Myrtle had been out so late the night before, when the phone rang.

It was Willow.

Myrtle's heart lurched when she heard Willow's voice. "I have this terrible feeling that Kojak is in Cullen's yard, Miss Myrtle. You know—tied to a tree. Whenever Jill wasn't there, Cullen tied him up. That's why I had to rescue him. And Red said Kojak had ended up back at Cullen's house again."

"What about Simon? Couldn't he take the dog?"

"Oh no, Miss Myrtle. Kojak *hates* Simon. He can take Miss Chivis, the cat, though. Can you make sure Libba gets the cat? I know she was real sick with cancer and all last year, but she seems better now. I think she can handle pet ownership."

"Yes, all right. And I remember you mentioning something about Simon and Kojak not getting along. Why is that, again?"

"Animals can just tell when someone doesn't like them. Simon doesn't like Kojak. I know it's a little bit of an imposition, especially considering last night," continued Willow shyly, "but I know how great you've been with your cat. I was wondering if you could just untie Kojak? Just let him loose in the yard. And make sure he has food and water out there? I really, really appreciate it."

Her train has missed the station. Attempts at murder one day, asking you to pet sit the next.

Still, it wasn't such a bad idea. Odd as it may seem, Myrtle didn't have a *done* feeling about the case. Yes, the killer was behind bars. But it felt like there was some sort of loose end—a bit of unresolved hate somewhere, maybe. And Myrtle was curious to see the dog that had helped spur Willow's hatred of Cullen.

Feeling a little like an animal rights activist from PETA, Myrtle opened the gate and looked around for Kojak. She stopped, frowning. She didn't see anything that looked like a Kojak. No big dogs. No small dogs, either. But she did hear a mournful baying inside Cullen's house. Apparently Cullen hadn't gotten around yet to chaining up the poor dog.

She'd come back by tomorrow and make sure Kojak wasn't chained up. Myrtle was just turning to slip back out the gate when she heard. "Whatchu doin' here, Miz Myrtle?"

Myrtle nearly jumped out of her skin before she realized it was just Tiny Kirk looming over her. "Tiny! You scared the fool out of me."

Tiny looked like he thought a Myrtle Clover minus the fool might be a vast improvement.

Myrtle saw that Tiny's truck with his yard equipment was in Cullen's driveway. "Oh. I guess you're here to clean up the yard."

Tiny nodded. "Mr. Caulfield hired me to clean it up, since Miz Caulfield was dead and can't cut the grass no more."

"I'm surprised Mr. Caulfield even *cares*," said Myrtle.

"Mr. *Simon* Caulfield hired me."

"Oh." Myrtle guessed Simon didn't want to be embarrassed by a veritable jungle in his brother's yard. Seeing that Tiny was still looking at her curiously, Myrtle added, "I was just here to let Kojak off the chain. But he's inside, judging from all the barking going on in there."

Tiny still looked puzzled—even more than was his natural expression.

"Willow called me and asked me to make sure the dog wasn't chained in the back yard," she finished lamely.

"Willow?" Tiny knit his brows and leaned forward over Myrtle as if to hear better. "I didn't know you were friends with Willow."

Neither did Myrtle.

"Well, yes, but she was worried about the dog. She knows that I ... care about animals."

Tiny gave his shaggy head a shake as if to clear it. "All I know, Miss Myrtle, is that I need that dog leashed up while I mow. At least he's not out here this time, but next time I'm going to have to chain him up if he's outside."

Myrtle was sick of the whole conversation by this time. "Well, can't you just let him off again when you're done?"

"That's no problem, Miz Myrtle."

Sherry appeared in the back yard with them. It was getting to be a regular party, Myrtle thought grimly. "Wonder what's wrong with Kojak?" she asked. "He never bays like that."

Myrtle shook her head and Sherry hesitated. "Maybe we should go in and check on him. Cullen's not used to taking care of the dog—maybe he's forgotten to feed him or let him out. Miss Myrtle, would you mind going in there with me?"

Myrtle was starting to think forward to a big cup of coffee and writing the front page exclusive. "I suppose we should," she said grudgingly. "But how will we get inside?"

"I've got a key," said Sherry. "I used to watch the animals for Jill and Cullen when they went out of town."

But Sherry didn't need her key because the door was unlocked. As soon as Sherry pushed it open, Kojak came charging out, howling balefully. Myrtle drew in a sharp breath. Kojak was spattered with blood. "He's hurt!" said Sherry, bending over to gently examine the basset hound, who looked nothing at all like a Kojak. Myrtle grimly continued walking into the house.

She froze when she found what she'd known she'd find as soon as she saw Kojak. It was Cullen, shot dead on his den floor. A revolver lay in his hand.

Myrtle turned around quickly to keep Sherry from following her into the den. But it was too late. "That's funny. Kojak doesn't seem to have a scratch on him—"she stopped short and stared at the body on the floor. And though Myrtle never would have pegged Sherry as a screamer, she started a horrific, hysterical shrieking that pierced the air as she took a few steps toward Cullen.

Myrtle grabbed her arm. "Sherry! Sherry, we can't touch him. We've got to stay back."

Sherry took her words to heart and ran *away* from the body, plowing back through the kitchen and out the backdoor, screaming all the way. Myrtle heard the lawnmower cut off in the backyard as Sherry's shrieks permeated the noise of the machine.

Myrtle knew she only had a couple of minutes at most to quickly look around before neighbors would be rushing in with Red hot on their tail. She put her hands behind her back so she wouldn't be tempted to touch anything and contaminate it and then glanced rapidly around the room.

It certainly *looked* like a suicide. Cullen had pulled the trigger in his mouth, with devastating consequences. The gun was right there in his hand. And, sure enough, there was a piece of white paper on the coffee table. Myrtle leaned over, holding on to her cane as she squinted at the printed text.

I killed Jill because I wanted to be with Sherry and couldn't afford a divorce. The guilt is killing me, though. I'm signing off. Cullen

Myrtle frowned. This wasn't right. Cullen *hadn't* killed Jill. And this didn't even sound like something that Cullen would write.

Unfortunately, one of the old biddies from across the street had immediately called the police as soon as she heard Sherry's screams. Since their neighborhood was on high alert, there was apparently a zero tolerance policy for early morning shrieking. Myrtle could already hear Red yelling in the yard, "Everybody get *back*. Move back to the sidewalk! Now!" Myrtle quickly backed away from the coffee table and Cullen's body and moved to the kitchen.

Red glowered at her as he pushed the backdoor open. "Mama! Why am I not surprised?"

"I can easily explain what I was doing here, Red. It's because of Kojak—the basset hound. Willow called me on the phone—"

Red held up a hand. "*Willow?* Can we talk about this later? And please go out to the sidewalk with everybody else in the neighborhood."

The scene outside was, in contrast to the stillness and quiet in Cullen's den, chaotic. Myrtle's cell phone started ringing as soon as she walked outside. "Miss Myrtle? Can you get over to Cullen Caulfield's house? Big story."

It was Sloan. Sloan's definition of a big story usually encompassed Frannie Brock's prize winning tomatoes. But this time he was right about the size of the story.

"I'm one step ahead of you today, Sloan. I discovered the body. With Sherry."

"You did *what*? Miss Myrtle! I could kiss you!"

"I can assure you that won't be necessary," said Myrtle. "And I have another big story for you, too—Willow tried to kill me last night. She was the murderer all along." She said this in a low voice as she slowly thumped her way back out to the sidewalk in front of the house.

"*What*?" Sloan's voice was absolutely delighted. Myrtle could tell he was already envisioning the headline on the front page.

"I'll tell you the whole story when I see you," said Myrtle. "There are too many people crowded around and I want them to read the story in the paper, not hear it from me while I'm blabbering on the phone to you."

Sloan gave a low whistle. "So it was Willow all the time. Of course, I've gotta get a stand-in for her—don't guess she'll be writing horoscopes anytime soon. You think you can get out of there and write me up a quick story? We could squeeze out a special edition of the paper before everyone hears the news about Willow. I can make some calls and maybe even get a couple of extra advertisers. Hmm." Sloan was already counting the dollars in his head.

"I'm going to probably be here for the next forty-five minutes or so. Red is probably going to want to question me about finding Cullen. But then I'll get right home and type you up a quick story."

Miles was already walking up along with several other neighbors, so Myrtle hung up while Sloan was still yammering about the article.

"Sherry said," murmured Miles, "that Cullen killed himself."

Myrtle shook her head, crossly. "No. Someone wanted us to *think* he killed himself."

"But she saw the gun in his hand."

"There's no *reason* for Cullen to have killed himself. Why would he do such a thing?"

"Maybe he was depressed. He seemed really guilty about cheating on Jill, especially since she died the day she found out. Maybe he couldn't stand the status quo anymore."

"That might be true, but he didn't *kill* himself," hissed Myrtle. "The suicide note? He confessed to killing Jill in it."

Miles gaped at her.

"Which means that someone killed Cullen before they found out Jill's murderer was Willow. Someone wanted to get rid of Cullen Caulfield and have it written off as the suicide of a guilty man. And I don't think that someone was Willow—the crime scene looked too recent for Willow to have done it. She spent the night in jail. Besides, Kojak wasn't going berserk for too many hours."

Miles started sputtering questions but Myrtle shushed him as Erma Sherman waddled up.

Erma gave Miles and Myrtle an oppressive group hug, knocking Myrtle's head into Miles's. Erma had now inserted herself in their tete-a-tete. "Isn't it *awful*?" asked Erma with obvious delight. "I guess Cullen couldn't live with himself anymore after killing Jill! And he killed himself!"

Myrtle frowned at her, which was her normal expression when dealing with Erma. "And where would you get an idea like that?" Myrtle gave Miles a repressing look.

"Well, Sherry told a bunch of us that he'd killed himself. I think Sherry believes he was upset over her dumping him." Erma laughed unpleasantly. "But it's clear *that* wasn't it. We all know that Cullen was the one who dumped *Sherry*, not the other way around. Cullen would just have moved on to the next pretty face. No, he killed himself because of guilt. He was wracked with it!" Erma's face lit up with the possibilities.

Myrtle gritted her teeth. How the hell did Erma know about Sherry and Cullen's relationship? It had taken her half the case to find out that the two of them were having a fling.

"Sherry will obviously need some grief counseling. People in Bradley will be sure to bring casseroles and condolences once they know how close Cullen and Sherry really were." A thoughtful look passed over Erma's face. "Don't you think we should have gun control in Bradley?" Erma asked. "Maybe Red can do something, Myrtle. He needs to do something about banning guns in Bradley. People should not be able to go around killing themselves here."

"Not," noted Myrtle through gritted teeth, "that Red has *anything* to do with *creating* laws, you know. He merely *enforces* them."

"Well maybe," said Erma after giving a sniff that turned more into a snort, "he should try to do more about it. Now Simon could be the next to go, you know. Grief-stricken over his brother's death."

Myrtle had to roll her eyes over that one. "Grief-stricken? Over Cullen?"

"He *was* his brother. All I'm saying," spat Erma, "is that we should consider banning guns in Bradley. Before we're all bleeding to death in the streets."

"There's a little matter of the second amendment to work around," said Miles dryly.

The Neanderthal-like hulk of Tiny Kirk loomed over Miles. "You with the NRA, Miles?"

"He probably is," grumbled Erma. "Doesn't want to ban guns."

"I didn't *say*—"groaned Miles.

"Ban guns?" asked Tiny with a barbaric yawp. "You want to ban guns?"

Tiny was well into a monologue on the glories of gun ownership and the wonders of hunting when he changed course into a diatribe against anti-gun people. "Like that what's-iz-name loudmouth at the party."

Who? thought Myrtle.

"Mr. Caulfield. He said no one should have guns in a house with young people."Tiny finished his tirade and stood, dejected. "And now it looks like the end of my grass-cutting days. Who knows when I'll get paid for last time?"

"Oh, I'm sure Simon is good about paying his bills."

Tiny shook his head vigorously. "He hired me, but he weren't gonna *pay* me. Said to bill Mr. Cullen for it."

"Oh. Well, that will be a problem. Maybe Simon will pay you after all."

"Doubt it. *He* don't have money, either." His prospects for payment diminishing, Tiny slumped. Tiny must really need the business. Myrtle made a mental note to keep him in mind if she ever got rid of the Puddin and Dusty package deal.

Miles frowned at her and gripped her elbow. "Do you need a hand, Myrtle? You're not looking too well. Where's your cane?" Erma was already excitedly darting over to another group of onlookers and spreading her bile.

Myrtle grimaced. Willow's phone call had knocked everything else out of her head. She must have forgotten to pick up her cane. "I've got to get out of here," she groaned. "If Red catches me without my stick, he'll check me into Greener Pastures Retirement Home before you can say boo."

"I've got my car," said Miles. "I can drop you off at your house. But don't you need to stay around and talk to the police?"

Myrtle waved her hand dismissively. "Red and Lieutenant Perkins know where to find me if they want to talk to me. I think yesterday knocked the stuffing right out of me. And I got up too early this morning, too. I'm going to put my feet up." Last night must have taken a bigger toll on her than she'd thought.

She'd walked in her door, taken off her shoes and thankfully lain down on her unmade bed when the phone rang. She sighed. Red had given her a cordless phone the previous Christmas, but it never seemed to stay where she could find it.

She walked into the living room but couldn't tell what direction the cordless phone's shrill was coming from. It seemed like the noise was coming from everywhere. Myrtle gave up and headed into the kitchen ... which was still a disaster from the night before. She grimaced and reached for the wall phone.

She listened into the receiver and said, "Hi Elaine."

"Myrtle? You sound awful!"

A wave of tiredness washed over Myrtle. "Actually, I'm tired, Elaine."

"Well of course you are!" A sympathetic Elaine gushed. "After almost getting murdered last night? And then practically tripping up over a body this morning? You need to take it easy. And you know," her voice dropped down as if someone could hear them talking, "he was murdered. But they made it look like suicide.

Red called me to say he was going to be awhile—that it was murder."

Myrtle's heart jumped. "I *knew* it. And Willow didn't do it, we know. She was already arrested!" She paused. "Unless Cullen was killed before nine o'clock last night."

Elaine said, "No, that's just it. The coroner thought it was after midnight. So Red and Lieutenant Perkins have to find out what's going on." Elaine stopped, as if suddenly realizing her gossip was probably counterproductive. "Hey, you should be putting your feet up, not rehashing everything with me."

Myrtle sighed. "Taking it easy sounds good. But I've got to clean up this poisoned casserole mess. I thought Forensics was going to scoop up everything, but they just took a sample and left everything else on the floor. I'm worried Pasha is going to slip in the door behind me some time and start eating it. God knows what's in it."

"Well, Jack is playing at his buddy's house. How about if I come over and give you a hand?" asked Elaine. "And maybe I can reset the trap for you, too."

"Thanks for offering, Elaine, but that's not the kind of thing you should be worrying about when you've got a few free minutes. Nor," she added hurriedly as Elaine's protests spilled out, "do *I* want to be bent over, scrubbing poisoned casserole off my kitchen floor. This," she concluded, "is a job for Puddin."

Elaine's voice sounded doubtful. "Are you sure? Puddin doesn't do a good job with anything, does she?"

"No. But this time might be the exception. I think her nose was really knocked out of joint when I hired Jill to do my cleaning for me. She might do an especially good job this time. For Puddin, anyway."

"Too bad the Jill thing didn't work out," said Elaine. "She was a cleaning whiz, wasn't she?"

"She was. But she snooped through my things. Puddin would *never* snoop. She just doesn't care that much ... about anything."

"I thought you'd called Puddin up and told her you were using Jill."

"It wasn't necessary. Puddin never shows up unless I call to harass her, anyway. She'd just take the opportunity to sit around watching her soaps all afternoon. But I'm sure she knew about Jill coming over. I saw Puddin in the Piggly Wiggly the other day and she stuck her nose up in the air and pretended she didn't see me. So she heard about it somehow."

"Well, if Puddin doesn't work out," said Elaine, "just call me up. If I can get melted crayon off the car seat, I can remove poisoned casserole from a kitchen floor."

"Thanks," said Myrtle. "I'm going to give Puddin a crack at it, though. Give her a chance to prove herself."

"And now," Myrtle said, "I'm going to write my big story."

Chapter Fifteen

Puddin entered Myrtle's house triumphantly, queen of all she surveyed and not a cleaning implement in sight. "At least I don't get myself murdered," she pointed out, proving she'd somehow known that Jill had been cleaning at Myrtle's. "You can count on me more than that." She ran her hand along a table top. There was very little dust there, although Myrtle hadn't done more than a little swipe since Jill last cleaned. "One of those freaky, obsessive-compulsive people, wasn't she? Got to have everything *perfect*." The last was uttered in a voice of snarling superiority.

"I could count on Jill to do a *good* job," said Myrtle repressively. "How do you know about obsessive compulsives, anyway?"

"Oprah reruns," drawled Puddin. At that moment, some odd backfiring noises emanated from Myrtle's front yard.

"What on earth is that?" breathed Myrtle. It sounded like an invasion.

"Dusty. He's mowin' the front yard."

"Well, how does he plan on doing that? I've got my gnomes out there!"

Puddin shrugged and pushed a strand of lank blonde hair off her round face. "Don't think you do, Miz Myrtle. Mr. Red gave Dusty some money to haul them back in the shed for you. Didn't want you to bust your back." When Myrtle's face flushed red with fury, Puddin added. "You wouldn't want your back thrown, Miz Myrtle. Lemme tell you," this as she took a seat on Myrtle's sofa, "that's just the worst feeling around. Can't clean, can't do nuthin'." She reached out for Myrtle's telephone. "Gotta make a quick call."

Myrtle wasn't sure which fire to put out first: the gnome-plucking, grass-hacking Dusty or the telephoning Puddin with no cleaning sprays. She decided to set things straight with Puddin once and for all. If they couldn't get off on the right foot this time, then it was time to find somebody else. Although that would mean shelling out more money, thought Myrtle uncomfortably. She'd really rather just keep who she had.

With that in mind, Myrtle said, "Puddin. No time to make calls. I need you to put on some gloves and throw away some food in the kitchen."

A startled look replaced the usually dour expression on Puddin's doughy face. She got off the sofa, and peered around the kitchen door. "Bless the good Lord. What happened here, Miz Myrtle?"

"Oh, Willow Pearce tried to kill me. That stuff has poison in it, Puddin, so handle it with respect. I don't have the time or energy today for your foolishness, so go ahead and take care of the mess. After that, you can wipe down the kitchen—it's okay to use my supplies this time, but I know you've got your own for next time. When Dusty is done with the yard, you can leave."

Puddin adopted her usual sullen look again. This was probably due to the fact that Dusty was notoriously poky with the yard work. Half the time was spent coaxing his ancient equipment to perform and half was spent trolling slowly around the yard, collecting his thoughts. Since he was her ride, Puddin usually spent the extra time resting her thrown back on Myrtle's sofa in front of her soaps. With her new regulations in place, Puddin plodded into the disorderly kitchen. She stopped short, gasped, and hurriedly made the sign of the cross.

"When did you become Catholic?" asked Myrtle with irritation. If Puddin had embraced "high church," the world really had turned upside down.

"It's a witch!" breathed Puddin.

"A witch?" Myrtle leaned forward on her cane and craned to look around Puddin's dumpy form. "Pasha!" Myrtle was alarmed to see the black cat in the kitchen. "Oh, you must have let her in when you poked your way in here. I hope she hasn't gotten into any of the food!"

Pasha glared at Myrtle for thinking her so ill-bred.

Puddin stammered. "That-that's a witch, Miz Myrtle."

Myrtle peered at Pasha. "No. It's a feline, Puddin."

"It's not! It's a witch in disguise. It'll bring horrible suffering on your home."

Pasha blinked at Puddin.

"Puddin, this is a cat. It's not, nor has it ever been a witch. It brings horrible suffering to the animal sacrifices she offers me and that's it." Myrtle was a bit pleased, however, by Puddin's antipathy to the cat. Maybe Pasha could also help keep Puddin in line.

Puddin reluctantly walked over to the sink and put on some latex gloves, keeping her eyes on the cat the entire time. "Mr. and Mrs. Caulfield have a black cat. And look what's happened to them."

Myrtle didn't answer for a moment and Puddin took that as her cue to start throwing away large clumps of vegetable casserole under the watchful eye of the black cat.

The problem with surviving several attempts on your life, thought Myrtle, was how darned overprotective everybody became. If Red had his way, she'd be wrapped up in cotton wool and packed away in Styrofoam peanuts. It was most disheartening for a star reporter-cum-sleuth.

The only way to really figure out what was going on was to get out and about. But any attempts to really do some investigating were bound to be foiled by Red and Perkins. No, it was going to take more ingenuity to be able to find out some useful information this time.

She thought about the remaining suspects. Georgia had still been angry at the time of Cullen's death over the lottery money she'd lost. Keeping that fact in mind, Myrtle had decided to use Georgia's affinity for angels to contact her again about the case. The motive was still there, after all.

The angels came in, as promised, on Wednesday—well-wrapped in protective bubble wrap, they seemed much nicer than anything anyone could get in Bradley. And cheaper too.

Perfect timing. Myrtle was keen to interview the elusive Georgia. Maybe she had some insight on Cullen's murder. She seemed well-versed in the philosophy of grudges, at any rate.

Thirty minutes later, Myrtle knocked at Georgia's ratty-looking door.

Georgia beamed when she saw Myrtle and the beam turned up a notch as her eyes rested greedily on the package of angels. Her eyebrows were a high arch, which gave her an appropriately surprised expression. "Come in, come in. Umm—want anything to drink, Miss Myrtle?"

Myrtle didn't. She had a feeling the kitchen matched the living room in its lack of cleanliness. And the living room's mess was of epic proportions. She was sure there *was* an angel collection somewhere in the heaps of paper, magazines, dirty plates, and laundry, but for the life of her, she couldn't see it. Maybe Georgia really did need an angel—a guardian one. Who liked to tidy up.

Myrtle said hurriedly, "I brought these over for you, Georgia. Found them in a back closet." No need to make her suspicious by telling her she'd ordered them off eBay. With expedited shipping.

Georgia picked one angel up, reverently. "These are really, really nice. I haven't seen any like these around." She wrinkled her brow. "How much do you want for them, Miss Myrtle?"

Myrtle waved her hands in a dismissive way. "Oh, nothing. You were nice enough to take the others off my hand. These are a gift. From a friend."

Georgia grinned. "Thank you so much, Miss Myrtle. That is really good of you."

Myrtle had no desire to embark on a long visit with Georgia in the depths of this black hole of debris.

Myrtle small-talked as much as she could bear, then said, "Isn't this awful business?" At Georgia's frown of confusion, Myrtle said, "Cullen's murder."

Georgia rolled her eyes and said tartly, "Or else he was just getting what he deserved."

Myrtle tried to look sympathetic.

Georgia continued, "See, I went over there. To Cullen's house." She dropped her voice as though her messy house had ears. "You know. To talk to him about the money. Make him see sense. See if he was as greedy as his wife was." She spat out the last few words.

"And when I got to his house, he was already deep in a squabble with somebody else. So he didn't get along with anybody real well, did he?"

"Who was he fighting with?" asked Myrtle.

"Sherry from next door. Don't know what that was all about. Well, talk was that they were having a fling, so maybe it had something to do with that. Sherry was right up in his face, yelling at him. Her face was red as a beet." Georgia touched her own powdered face as if reassuring herself it was its usual pasty color.

"Then what happened?"

"Sherry saw me and stomped off back to her house. Cullen went inside his house, too. Until I knocked on his door." Georgia pursed her lips. "He came flying out the door then. I guess he thought it was Sherry again. But he wasn't happy to see me, either. *And*," her ferocious brows drew down into a bunch, "he laughed at me when I asked him for the lottery money. *Laughed* at me!" Georgia fumed silently, apparently lost in her own angry world.

"Imagine that." Myrtle clucked. "So did you go back and kill him later?"

Georgia's black eyebrows went up almost to her hairline. She leaned forward to see if Myrtle was making fun of her. Apparently satisfying herself that she wasn't, Georgia considered the question. "Well, what's the real sin? Actually having the gumption to do something, or just wishing it would happen? I guess I sinned in my heart, but no I didn't kill him. Glad somebody did, though." Georgia patted an angel, remorsefully.

Myrtle wondered how much longer she should let this visit go on to keep Georgia from suspecting her detecting. She didn't really think she could stand it much longer. At least she'd gotten some information from her foray into the paper jungle. She reached for her pocketbook, but sat back abruptly when Georgia gushed, "You have to stay and have a coffee with me. You were just too sweet to bring me the angels!"

Myrtle gave a weak smile. Then she noticed the surface that was underneath the piles of magazines and unopened mail in front of her. "Is that ... ?"

Georgia beamed. "A coffin! I got it at a yard sale. The owner's son had made it for her, and then she ended up beating that cancer with a stick. So I got the coffin for five bucks! Isn't it a beaut? I'm going to use it for a coffee table until I need one. May as well get my money's worth out of it."

Myrtle's complete loss for words must have somehow translated into admiration. Georgia said, "You love it, don't you? I get *so* many comments on it from my visitors. I ended up tracking down the woman's son, who's an expert woodsman. I could get him to make you one if you like. You might not get as much time out of it as I will, considering your age and everything, but it would make a nice bookcase for all those books you have lying around. He could put some shelves in it, then Red could have them taken out when it's time for you to be buried."

Myrtle started twitching.

"Coffee!" said Georgia, snapping her fingers. "I know caffeine withdrawal when I see it. Be back in a jiff."

Myrtle was clearly being punished for something.

Chapter Sixteen

As much as Myrtle hated to admit it, she was ready to return to Fit Life. Her disturbing conversation with Georgia had gotten her thinking about coffins, a subject she didn't fancy. She'd suddenly gotten imbued with the foreign desire to exercise. This was coupled with an interest in talking with Sherry again and finding out Sherry's thoughts on Cullen's sudden death.

This time Myrtle walked straight back to the exercise equipment after waving a "hello" to Sherry on the way in. Myrtle gently worked out her arms on the weight machines, making sure to take the prescribed breaks in between sets. She finished up her exercise session with twenty minutes on the treadmill. It surprised her that she felt energized instead of tired after her workout.

It was a good time to catch up with Sherry. There was a lull in the gym and Sherry actually appeared not to be doing anything at the front desk. Myrtle was pleased when she called out to her.

"Miss Myrtle, I wanted to thank you for going in with me to Cullen's house. It was so horrible finding him that way." Sherry swallowed, putting her hand to her throat as if she were helping along the swallowing process. "I didn't sleep most of the night last night. And then, when I did? I had the most awful nightmares ever. Were you the same way?"

Myrtle shifted guiltily. She was up a lot last night, but she hadn't lost the sleep over Cullen's death. It was just her usual insomnia biting her in the rear end.

"Yes. I ... didn't sleep a wink last night," she said truthfully.

Sherry rushed around the desk and gave Myrtle a tight hug. "You poor thing. I hate that I asked you to go in with me and we had to see ... *that. Him*." She pulled a well-worn tissue out of her pocket and blew her nose on it. "I should have asked that stupid Tiny to go in with me. I should have known something was wrong, with Kojak so upset."

Myrtle, who usually would have snapped someone's head off at being called a 'poor thing' resisted the impulse. "What really made me sad was Kojak being so devastated and upset at Cullen's death, and Cullen hadn't apparently given a flip about the dog."

Sherry nodded. "Cullen wasn't an animal person. He wasn't a lot of things, actually," said Sherry with a short laugh. "Wasn't much of a worker. Wasn't much of a husband. But for some reason," she said, looking around her, "I really liked him. There wasn't any sense in it. But something about him drew me in."

Although Myrtle found the idea of being drawn to Cullen Caulfield about as appealing as necking with a gorilla, she summoned up her best sympathetic face.

"And Miss Myrtle?" Now Sherry was gripping Myrtle's arm tightly. "Somebody did him in. And it wasn't me!" She squeezed Myrtle's arm even tighter and Myrtle grunted.

"Well of *course* you didn't do it," said Myrtle. She pulled her arm away from Sherry and rubbed it. "No one's saying you did, are they?"

"Red is. Red thinks I did it—that I walked into Cullen's house, put the gun in his hand while he was drunk out of his mind, and pulled the trigger." She dug around for the tatty tissue and Myrtle offered her a clean one from her pocketbook. "But I didn't. You need to tell him. Tell him that I loved Cullen and would never have killed him." Her voice was a hoarse croak and Myrtle bit back some choice profanity as Sherry grasped her arm again.

"Why on earth would Red suspect you? Nobody knew about you and Cullen, right?" Except for Erma. And Simon. And Myrtle and Miles.

"That Georgia Simpson," said Sherry. "She told Red and that other cop that Cullen and I had an argument before he died. Arguments with murdered people really put a person on a cop's radar."

"Why were you arguing?"

"We were just never in sync. First of all he was hounding me to see him and I didn't want anything to do with him. Then I gave in. Cullen started feeling really guilty about our relationship—that he had been cheating on Jill the day she died. He was calling our relationship off." Bright red streaks of color covered Sherry's cheeks. "But he didn't mean it. It was just the guilt talking. He *loved* me," said Sherry in a fierce voice. Myrtle wondered if she'd told *Cullen* that in the same tone.

"You don't think he was missing Jill? Or something like that?" Myrtle looked innocent again.

Sherry made a face. "Maybe he missed having Jill clean for him and cook for him and do yard work for him. But he was willing to just let it all go to pot and live in the mess. His brother was disgusted enough with the yard to set up yard service for him, even though Simon doesn't have two dimes to rub together.

"But I do think Cullen felt *guilty* about Jill. He felt bad that he treated her like dirt right up until the night she died. But even feeling guilty and even with the booze, Cullen would never have pulled a trigger and killed himself. I know somebody killed him. I just have a gut feeling. And from the questions the cops were asking me, *they're* suspicious he was murdered, too."

Sherry looked around quickly again, but the lull of traffic at the gym continued. "I bet I know who *did* do it. I saw Blanche going in Cullen's house just the other day. And you know she and Jill were having some major squabble with each other? Well, the dog, Kojak, was going nuts *then*, too. When Blanche was in there visiting with Cullen. They must have been having one heck of an argument. She should feel ashamed of herself. Jill is dead and Blanche didn't act anything but hateful to her."

Myrtle tactfully refrained from mentioning the fact that Sherry had contributed greatly to the overall poor treatment of Jill. "Did you hear anything that night or that morning that Cullen was killed?"

Now Sherry frowned. "You mean, the gun going off? No, I sure didn't. I have one of those white noise machines that blocks out noise. I got it when Jill started all the crazy noisy Christmas music and then got used to it and never turned it off. That night I just took a warm bath after a bad day at work, crawled in the bed and crashed."

Sherry said in a strident voice. "He was going to come back to me, Miss Myrtle. We had something really special. And I just can't believe he's gone."

She finally let go of Myrtle's arm. "Anyway," she gave a hoarse laugh, "Enough of that. We'll both be having more nightmares if I keep talking about this stuff. Let's change the subject. Are you enjoying your new membership, Miss Myrtle?" Sherry had a smug look on her face as if she already knew the answer.

"Yes, all right, you were right, Sherry. Exercising can be addictive. I've been bitten by the bug."

"Well, if you have to have an addiction, at least that's a healthy one to have. I think your body just gets used to the endorphins and craves more."

The Fit Life door opened and a few customers walked in. "I'd better go, Miss Myrtle," said Sherry. "Good talking to you."

"I hate to admit it," said Myrtle in a confidential tone, "But exercising at Fit Life is proving surprisingly satisfying." She'd decided to walk over to Elaine and Red's house and have some refreshments after her exercising.

Elaine blinked. "I'm glad to hear it, Myrtle. I'm *shocked* to hear it, actually, but it's good news. I know it's got to be great for you, too."

Myrtle wagged a finger at Elaine, "Don't go tattling on me to Red. I don't need him meddling in my business any more than he already is."

"Myrtle, it was really your own idea to work out. Red made the suggestion after your physical, but he didn't push you to do it. So you can pat yourself on the back."

Myrtle said, "It's also made me reevaluate what else I might be missing out on that I should try to get involved in."

"Maybe Friends of Ferals? It sounds like you've enjoyed your interactions with your furry friend."

Myrtle made a face. "Sorry to crush your enthusiasm, Elaine, but I don't think I want to attend a bunch of meetings with rabid animal lovers like Willow."

Elaine rolled her eyes. "Myrtle, it's not like that. It's very civil and we always have food and drinks at our meetings. They're in someone's home. It's actually a lot more civil than supper club."

"Well, I would hope so, considering people get murdered at supper club." Elaine opened her mouth to further promote Friends of Ferals cause when Myrtle said quickly, "No, I was thinking more along the lines of going to church."

Since Elaine's mouth was already open to talk, it dropped even more at Myrtle's mention of church. Again.

"I know you and Red go every Sunday with Jack. Can you swing by and pick me up this Sunday?"

Elaine just nodded wordlessly. It had been shocking enough that Myrtle had wanted to attend the church luncheon. Wanting to attend a service was absolutely unheard of. In fact, she quoted Emily Dickinson whenever Red questioned her about going. Apparently Emily believed that you could worship God just as well in your own garden as in a manmade sanctuary. But then, Emily Dickinson was basically a recluse.

"It's not like I don't ever go to church, you know, Elaine. I was there just last week, remember?"

"You mean for the United Methodist Women luncheon? Myrtle, you were there to investigate a murder, as I recall."

"I was not." Myrtle sniffed. "I was there to show Red that I do have some inkling of civic involvement. That he doesn't *need* to sign me up for the Kiwanis pancake breakfast because I'm already involved in the community. Anyway," Myrtle attempted a dignified rise from the sofa, but it was completely spoiled by the depth of the furniture. She bounced several times until she was able to get up. " ... if you could pick me up on Sunday, that would be great."

Myrtle finally took pity on Elaine's confusion. "I'm trying some different things, that's all. It's not good to get stale, you know. So I'm trying out some new things to see what might suit me best—exercise, blogging, cooking—even church."

"Of course I'll pick you up," said Elaine, handing Myrtle her cane and watching out the window as she walked back home. She wasn't going to have Myrtle's immortal soul hanging on *her* conscience. Elaine would get her to church, by golly.

Church, thought Myrtle, wasn't all it's cracked up to be. Myrtle, a big fan of slacks and pant suits, had had a difficult time putting on the elderly pair of panty hose that she kept especially for church occasions. She hadn't worn the dress for a while and hadn't realized there was a button missing from the front. Once she'd finally replaced the button, gotten on the troublesome hose, and made a stab at applying makeup, she got into Elaine's van and was flummoxed that Elaine had on slacks. She was even more chagrined when she walked into the church and saw that nearly every woman there was wearing dress slacks. It *had* been a while since she'd been to a service.

Elaine walked over to her usual pew, but Myrtle patted her arm and said, "If it's all right with you, Elaine, I think I'm going to sit near the front." At Elaine's questioning look, Myrtle said, "You know ... I can see and hear a little better."

Elaine wasn't aware that Myrtle had any impediment at all to her sight or hearing. Maybe she was avoiding Red, although Red was just a "maybe" for the service, depending on if he were able to pull away from work in time.

Myrtle found that seating herself in church wasn't as easy as it appeared. When she tried the third row pew, Fritzie Cochran quickly pulled a sweater across the space Myrtle was planning on parking herself. Saving seats was one of those things that annoyed Myrtle. The person you're saving it for shouldn't be such a slowpoke and sit in their own place.

Her next attempt to sit down went just as poorly. Apparently, the second row pew was completely reserved, although there wasn't a sign at the end of the pew to say so. Several people looked coldly at her as she stood there, so she gave it a pass. She was just at the point of going back to sit with Elaine when she noticed a spot on the very first pew. Ordinarily she would have avoided sitting right under the minister's nose, but desperate times called for desperate measures.

The front row seemed to be designed for the old lady parishioners. There were devices on the pews for the hard of hearing. There were large print hymnals and Bibles. And, proving the point that old ladies were intended to worship there, there were three elderly ladies sitting very close together as if they were trying to warm their old bones by body heat in the chill of the sanctuary.

Myrtle, of course, knew these ladies. The town of Bradley was only so big, after all. Although she was actually older than a couple of them, she was a lot more mobile than they were. Actually, she might be a whole lot more compos mentis than these ladies, too. They sat together, shoulder to shoulder, but didn't say a word to each other, as if the process of getting ready for church had completely drained them. Or maybe, thought Myrtle, after all the years of coming to church every Sunday, they'd merely run out of conversation.

They merely nodded a recognition that Myrtle was joining them before easing back again into their quiet reflection. Or maybe, thought Myrtle, they were sleeping. One of them gave a little gasp of a snore, just confirming her suspicions that there was more napping than praying going on.

Myrtle glanced at her watch. There was no way that she was going to be able to sit quietly for twenty minutes while waiting for the service to start. She leaned closer to Coraline Walker and murmured, "Quite a week, hasn't it been?"

Coraline apparently didn't hear her.

"Quite a week, wasn't it?" asked Myrtle a little louder.

There was still no response and now Myrtle was concerned enough to tap Coraline insistently on her tiny leg. She hadn't passed through to the other side, had she?

Coraline's rheumy eyes rolled Myrtle's way.

"I said," Myrtle put her mouth right up at Coraline's ear, "that it was quite a week, wasn't it?"

Coraline considered for a moment. Then she bobbed her head very slightly and retreated back into her own private sanctuary.

Eva Jackson next to Coraline had apparently been able to hear Myrtle. She had been a schoolteacher at the same time Myrtle had taught, so they were acquainted with each other. Although the noise in the school cafeteria had been so loud that Myrtle doubted they'd ever held a proper conversation with each other.

Myrtle was certain she heard a rusty, creaking sound when Eva's mouth opened. Myrtle leaned over Eva's limp figure, expecting to have to strain to catch whatever sound trickled out. Instead, she recoiled when a bellowing bark came out. Apparently she was used to yelling at her nearly deaf companions.

"Saving your soul, Myrtle?" she hollered.

Myrtle scowled. She'd rather not have her poor church attendance blasted out to the congregation. "You know I come to church, Eva. I just usually sit in the back and you don't see me."

"Hogwash!" And then, abruptly changing subjects, "That poor girl!" she roared. "And now I don't have anyone to clean for me. Do you like your girl?"

"Puddin isn't really someone I can recommend. But she's cheap, if that's what you're looking for. Or if you don't care about dust elimination."

"Dead as a doornail! Can you believe it?"

Myrtle was somewhat used to abrupt subject changes with her contemporaries, so this non sequitur didn't throw her as much as it might other people. "Jill? Yes, she is, I'm afraid."

"And the scoundrel," barked Eva.

"Cullen? Yes."

Eva nodded to herself and pursed her lips in thought. Her friends sat on either side of her, totally expressionless. "Those boys never did get along."

Now Myrtle was having to work a bit harder to follow Eva's thought patterns. "Boys?"

"The brothers. Hated each other. No wonder he did him in."

Myrtle frowned. "You think Simon Caulfield killed his brother?" They'd definitely been slugging it out at the gym, but murder was completely different.

"Half-brother. Remember? And yes, of course he did." Now Eva Jackson was squinting at Myrtle as if she was concerned about her mental faculties.

"But *why*?"

"Because they hated each other!" Now Eva looked merely irritated. She sniffed and leaned back onto the pew. "I'll call her."

Myrtle assumed she meant Puddin and not the murdered Jill. She wasn't ready to give up on the conversation, but at that moment the organ boomed and she gave up on any further attempts.

Chapter Seventeen

Puddin was half-heartedly vacuuming Myrtle's living room carpet when the phone rang. A look of relief passed over her face when Myrtle put a finger up to her lips and grabbed the phone. Instead of moving on to some other housework, Myrtle noticed that Puddin plopped down on the sofa to listen in.

It was Blanche on the line. "Since you've been involved recently with the United Methodist Women," said Blanche (did Myrtle imagine the faint emphasis on 'recently'?), "I wonder if you would be available to help out today."

Myrtle hemmed and hawed. Had it come to this, then? Was she going to be stuck doing good works all over Bradley? "Well ... " she started in a doubtful way.

"It's to help out Libba. Libba Caulfield?"

"What's wrong with Libba Caulfield? Her cancer hasn't come back for sure, has it?" asked Myrtle. Puddin leaned forward on the edge of the sofa.

Blanche answered with her usual restraint and understatement. "I'm not sure about the cancer. I'm hoping she's still in remission, since she's been doing so well the last few years. But she's been doing poorly since Cullen's death. The United Methodist Women thought it would be helpful for us to stop by for a visit."

Puddin rolled her eyes and muttered loudly to herself in the background. Myrtle waved a hand at her, repressively. "I'd be happy to visit Libba, Blanche. Five o'clock? See you then." She replaced the phone receiver and glared at Puddin.

"What was all that muttering about, Puddin? You're supposed to be worrying about my floors."

Puddin bobbed her head sagely. "But that was Blanche? Calling about Miz Caulfield going all wacky, I guess."

"And what do you know about it?" asked Myrtle. Although, she thought, Puddin should be well qualified to recognize wackiness.

"She thinks the family is cursed," said Puddin. "And the curse has stricken her." Puddin gave a vindictive nod.

"Are you sure, Puddin?" Myrtle squinted her eyes suspiciously. "Blanche just hinted that Libba was under the weather."

"*Under* the weather?" Puddin snorted. "Not just under it. Struck down by it!"

Puddin was getting on a roll. Sensing Puddin had a heretofore unknown melodramatic flair, Myrtle shrugged and started going off to do her business.

Puddin stopped her. "I go there to clean, you know. Well, I did a couple of times, when Libba Caulfield was sick. Then they had Jill over to clean for a while, I guess because she was family. Then they had *me* come back after Jill was dead."

Puddin sounded grimly satisfied. Myrtle was beginning to wonder if she should add Puddin to the list of suspects. Her work load had certainly improved since Jill's death.

Myrtle found it hard to believe that Simon Caulfield would put up with Puddin's foolishness.

"And Miz Caulfield's gone off the deep end. She's nuttier than a fruitcake."

"And why is that?"

"The Caulfields are cursed, ain't they?" Puddin gave a vindictive nod.

"Well, Jill and Cullen maybe. I don't think there's an evil spirit that's annihilating the whole family or anything."

Puddin mulled over the "annihilate." Then she shrugged. "Miz Caulfield seems to think so. Rumor has it (Myrtle had a strong feeling that Puddin was behind this particular rumor) that she's a step away from puttin' herself out of her misery."

"Sure she is."

"It's a fact!" Puddin took a deep breath and added, "Besides, they're in awful shape, you know. Mr. Caulfield had to let me go that very day. Said they couldn't afford to have me clean for them anymore. They never did seem to pay me on time, but I was happy to go over there and help them out, even though they didn't really pay." Puddin adopted an angelic stance. The Selfless Puddin. "And I know they have trouble paying their bill at the grocery store, too, because that's where my cousin Bitsy works." Puddin had various and sundry cousins all over Bradley and they all gossiped voraciously.

But Myrtle wasn't really even listening. Wouldn't Simon Caulfield be expecting his brother's money to be willed to him on his death? If the Caulfields were having trouble paying bills, if they were worried about upcoming medical expenses, and if Simon or Libba knew that Jill had some money from the lottery ... .and *if* they knew they'd be the beneficiaries ... It added up to a motive in Myrtle's eyes. A motive, but that was it. She couldn't go to the police with just the idea. She'd have to do some nosing around. It would make another blockbuster front page story.

"Get back to your cleaning, Puddin. I've got some cooking to do."

Myrtle walked into her kitchen with her hands on her hips. She'd go to Libba Caulfield's house with a casserole in hand. And it was going to be the best darned casserole anyone had ever tasted. So what if the last time she'd tried to cook while reading the food blog hadn't worked out so well? At least she'd been cooking for herself. Besides, it hadn't been *her* fault. It was Sloan's. Sloan hadn't told her how addicting blog reading could be. You jump from link to link and click around and end up on the most random and interesting stuff, and next thing you know your chicken casserole is burned to a crisp. Thank heavens for the

Piggly Wiggly. Too bad Erma had been such a know-it-all and blabbed about the casserole's origins.

This time would be better. She was going to actually prepare a casserole, put it in the oven, set the *timer*, and then step away from the computer. She pulled up her browser and typed in a site.

The scene at the Caulfields was an odd one. Myrtle perched uncomfortably on the edge of an elderly, overstuffed sofa with a floral motif. Blanche, if possible, looked even more uncomfortable in a straight backed chair. The lady of the house was a bona fide wreck of a woman, sporting a spotty bathrobe that had seen better days. Not an ounce of makeup assisted Libba's pinched features. The overwhelming habit of being a decent hostess came briefly to the forefront and Libba asked them if they wanted a glass of sweet tea.

They turned it down. Lord, who knew how long it might have been since she'd whipped up that batch? It might have been before Jill's death. That pitcher could be teeming with creepy-crawlies.

Libba hadn't even turned a hair when Myrtle brought in her casserole. That right there, Blanche later told Tippy, was a sure sign of mental weakness. Any *normal* person would have turned at least a *little* green when presented with a genuine Myrtle Clover casserole.

Myrtle was also sure there was something wrong with Libba, but for different reasons. She'd known Libba Caulfield since she was a wee thing and she'd never seen her forget her manners. Libba was always the type to take it a step farther, too. She'd rise when elderly ladies came into the room, and it was said that she set a beautiful table when she had dinner guests. She was a closet *Amy Vanderbilt's Complete Book of Etiquette* reader, Myrtle was sure. The untidy, hollow-eyed woman she saw today bore no resemblance to the Libba Caulfield she knew.

When Simon walked into the room, stopped abruptly and took in his company with angry eyes, Myrtle nearly didn't recognize him, either. He was always neatly dressed, but today looked downright scruffy. Although the Caulfields were supposed to be having financial problems, they always did look neat and rather like what you'd think troubled gentility would look like. Simon had a large gash on his leg that he'd tried to cover with a bandage. If he'd *really* wanted to hide it, he should have skipped the shorts.

"What happened to you, Simon? Looks like something tried to eat you." Myrtle peered closely at his leg.

Simon held his mouth so tight that there was a white line on either side of it. "I ... had a problem with the lawnmower a couple of days ago."

"But Tiny cut the grass then."

Simon made an impatient swipe with his hand. "Well, whenever I last cut it or did the edging. Anyway, it's nothing." As if suddenly realizing that his guests were hardly the recipients of gold star hosting, he said, "Thanks for coming by. It's been ... a rough couple of days." He spoke the words grimly and looked quickly over at Libba who had slipped back into her funk.

Blanche was having a hard time keeping her eyes off of Libba. The transformation was pretty alarming, thought Myrtle. "Is there anything we can do?" asked Blanche. "Besides the casseroles. This must be such a horrible time for you."

Libba looked blankly back at Blanche so Simon stepped in. "Blanche, would you mind very much helping Libba back to the bedroom? Putting her feet up for a little while might be the best medicine for her."

A relieved expression passed across Blanche's face, "Of course I will. Libba?" And she and Libba disappeared into the back of the house.

Simon stared uncomfortably at the floor for a silent minute while he looked to be coming up with something to talk about. Myrtle, on the other hand, was happy to keep the silence going. She'd learned, in the course of her investigations, that uncomfortable silences were wonderful for spurring on surprising conversations.

Simon cleared his throat. "Miss Myrtle, I saw that story of yours in the newspaper the other day. You've become quite the investigative reporter." This was said in a tone such as one would use to convey praise on a child.

Myrtle managed a tight smile. "Yes. I'm sorry about the subject matter of the story, though. I know it must have been hurtful to your family to read about Willow and Jill."

Simon waved his hand in a dismissive gesture. "The truth had to come out. It was a shock, though. I'd never have thought that Willow would have killed her own sister. It's just been one tragedy after another."

"I'm so sorry about Cullen. I know that's been another horrible shock."

"It's so hard for me to grasp that Cullen would have been depressed enough to kill himself like that," said Simon. "I wish he'd have felt like he could come to me and talk. I always told him that guns were dangerous things."

"But you two didn't talk much, did you?" Simon shot her a look and Myrtle continued. "I mean, you never did get along well. Even when you were boys."

"Brothers are like that," said Simon in a distracted voice. "Speaking of not getting along, I was surprised to see Blanche here." His voice was hushed. "I'd gone by to check on Cullen a few days after Jill died. She did everything for him," he gave a derisive snort, "so I wanted to make sure that he was at least capable of feeding himself with Jill gone. I think he'd been living on frozen waffles. When I opened up the door, I heard Blanche and Cullen fighting with each other."

Myrtle drew in her breath and nodded encouragingly to Simon.

"I slipped back out again before they saw me. It sounded like ... well, it sounded like Cullen was trying to blackmail Blanche and that she was trying to talk sense into him. I hate to think that my own brother would do something like that. But it might be something I should tell Red about." He looked as though the words left a nasty aftertaste in his mouth.

"Does it really matter now?" asked Myrtle innocently. "Since Cullen is dead, his plan is over, isn't it? If it had been murder, then we'd definitely want to let Red know. But with it being suicide ... And you are sure it was suicide?"

"Aren't you? You were there with Sherry when you saw the scene. Sherry said there was a gun in his hand."

"And a note on the table," nodded Myrtle.

"Did you have a chance to read the note?" asked Simon intently. "The police haven't released it yet. I think it would give me –some comfort—to know what was going through Cullen's mind."

"I did read it," said Myrtle. "It was just right there next to me." She opened her mouth, but shut it again at the sound of footsteps coming from the hall.

"I'll call you later," said Simon quickly, clearly not wanting to discuss the note in front of Blanche.

Blanche looked tired as she joined them. "I think she's going to sleep now. Maybe a short nap will do her some good. Myrtle? Are you ready to head on?'

Blanche didn't say much as they got into the car and drove off. Myrtle said, "Blanche, I've been meaning to ask you how *you* are doing."

Blanche didn't pretend not to know what Myrtle was talking about. "Much better. It's like night and day. I talked to my doctor and am going to get some treatment for the prescription drug problem. And—it sounds awful to say it, but life really started looking up as soon as Jill died."

"It doesn't sound awful at all, considering she was blackmailing you. You couldn't exactly be expected to be sobbing at her funeral."

Blanche took a deep breath. "And then things crashed downhill again last week. Cullen called me over to the house and I knew what must have been on his mind if he was asking to see me. It's not like we were friends." The idea of a friendship with Cullen made Blanche look revolted. "Sure enough, as soon as I knocked on his door, he was asking for money. I guess that was the only way he could think of to make some money, since he sure wasn't going to haul his lazy rear end out to look for a job."

"What happened?"

"I was just fed up. He planned on keeping up with Jill's little blackmailing gig and thought I'd just pony up the money like a little lamb. But I'd had it. Besides, I was already getting treatment. I was already recovering—it was old news. And, like you mentioned, Myrtle, everyone pulls for the underdog—it's not as if I were still an addict. So I told him off. Told him I didn't care who he told—and wasn't it the pot calling the kettle black for an alcoholic to blab about a prescription drug addict?"

Blanche looked just as furious now as she must have looked that evening. Then she settled down. "But I didn't kill the man. He didn't have any more power over me, so why would I? Besides, the dog started going berserk so I looked at it as a good time to leave."

They pulled up in Myrtle's driveway and Myrtle said as she stepped out the door, "I'm really happy for you, Blanche. I know how tough it's got to be to get better from an addiction. I'm pulling for you."

"Myrtle, believe me, things are really starting to look up."

After a little reading and a short nap, Myrtle started feeling a little hungry. She realized that in her concentration to produce a wonderful casserole for the Caulfields, that she'd forgotten to feed herself. Myrtle peered doubtfully into her fridge, then opened her pantry. Not only did everything look unappealing, the assorted ingredients didn't seem like they'd add up to a meal. Every recipe she could think of was missing at least one major component. She was even out of cereal and grits. She sighed. Maybe cheese biscuits and grapes would make a decent supper. She'd get Red to take her to the store tomorrow.

The mind-boggling thing to Myrtle was that the Caulfield's kitchen was in much the same state. Libba would never ordinarily allow her supplies to get so low. And she wouldn't be the horrible hostess as she'd been earlier. Maybe Puddin was actually right for once and Libba was losing the use of her mind. She definitely hadn't been this bad off when she'd been sick several years ago. You'd hardly have known she was ill with cancer at all—she was so on top of things, even when she was in the bed. Jotting down who'd brought in casseroles, or come by for a visit. And you'd always get the nicest, most well-bred thank you note from her.

Simon's behavior wasn't all that normal, either. And what was the deal with the huge gash on his leg and his secretive manner?

Myrtle heard dogs barking outside and looked out her window. She hoped Pasha was okay. Funny how that cat was growing on her.

The dogs continued barking in what seemed like a domino effect from one yard to the next. It was like the Hounds of the Baskervilles out there. Myrtle gave a gasp. What about Kojak? Now that Cullen was dead, there wasn't anyone over there to take care of the poor dog. Willow was in jail and she'd said that Kojak hated Simon, so the dog couldn't go to the other Caulfields. Maybe she should call up Red and see if the police had taken the dog to the shelter.

Myrtle frowned. Wait a minute. There was something in that line of thought that she needed to explore. What was it? Kojak. It all came together quickly.

Her thoughts were rudely interrupted by the acrid smell of smoke coming from the direction of her kitchen. The biscuits! Myrtle hurried into the kitchen, shoved open a window, turned off the oven, and pulled out the biscuits, which now strongly resembled lumps of charcoal. Shoot! Now what was she going to eat?

The knock at her back door made her jump. She hoped whoever it was wasn't hungry. And that she could get rid of the person quickly so she could make her victorious phone call to Red and let him know she'd solved the case.

She opened the door a crack. "Miss Myrtle," said Simon Caulfield, "I thought we could talk a little about that suicide note now."

"I know I said I'd talk to you about it later, Simon, but it's going to have to wait. I've got this important phone call that I'm making." She firmly pushed on the door to close it again, then desperately shoved at it as Simon applied his own considerable strength to the other side.

With another shove, he'd pushed his way through. "No, I think now is a good time to visit," he said in a hard voice. And Myrtle realized he held a knife in his hand.

Chapter Eighteen

Myrtle swallowed hard. "I suppose so, If you really want to visit, Simon. How's that leg of yours doing? That's a nasty bite Kojak gave you."

Simon growled, "Stupid dog. I knew you'd figured out I killed Cullen when you were looking at my leg."

"Willow told me that Kojak hated you. And I knew you were lying about cutting Cullen's grass because I saw Tiny Kirk doing yard work there the day of Cullen's murder. But you're wrong—I didn't put it all together until right before you walked through my door." She summoned up the old schoolteaching voice that used to have a quelling effect on Simon in the classroom. "This is stupid, Simon. Put that knife down. You're only adding to your problems."

He shook his head, emphatically. "Math never was your strong suit, Miss Myrtle. I'm thinking if I get rid of you now then I'm actually subtracting from my problems. Everyone thinks Cullen killed Jill, either in a drunken rage or because he wanted to be free to marry someone else and couldn't afford a divorce. And then Cullen conveniently killed himself out of guilt. But you ... " now his voice snarled, "had to start nosing around. Why'd you care? What possible difference could it make to you?"

"The police already knew it was murder," said Myrtle, shifting her weight onto her cane. They knew right away, because of the note you wrote. None of this is my fault, Simon. It's your fault for writing the suicide note you did. It's your fault for being on bad terms with Kojak. And it's your fault for killing your brother." Myrtle was going to talk as much and as long as she could. The more she talked, the better a chance she had at getting out of this fix.

"My brother." Simon laughed brokenly. "Half-brother by blood and never a real brother to me in any sense of the word."

"I remember when you were both in school together," mused Myrtle. "You were always the dutiful older brother, weren't you? Always doing your homework, making good grades. And Cullen … ."

"Cullen was a loser. As always." Simon's voice was harsh. "He never did anything he was supposed to do. He cheated his way through school, and people always, *always* liked him. Our dad *loved* him." He stopped abruptly. Myrtle looked closely at him. It looked like he was choking back tears.

"Surely he loved you, too?" said Myrtle, leading him on.

"No! He never did. And when dad got sick, Cullen got to him with his lies. He told Dad that I … "

Myrtle's mind whirled. What kind of lie was guaranteed to upset Joel Caulfield the most about his son? Drugs? That he'd gotten some girl pregnant? That he didn't want to join the family business? Then she had an idea. "He told your father you were gay. That would have been the unforgivable sin for Joel Caulfield, wasn't it? To him that would have been a direct slap at *him*. It would have undermined his own masculinity, and that was very important to him. I remember he was a big athlete and outdoorsman."

Simon's eyes glittered. "It was all a lie. Cullen knew Dad would disown me and he could take the inheritance for himself. And that's what happened."

"And it's been eating away at you for years," said Myrtle. "You hated your brother for that, didn't you?"

"Not only did he turn my father against me, but he took the money that should have been mine and drank it away." Simon spat the words out.

"Did your wife know you felt this way?" Myrtle did want to know. But she was even more interested in stalling Simon. Was there any way she could use her cane to dislodge the knife?

The mention of his wife erased some of the lines on Simon's face. "Libba didn't know anything about it," he said. "She would just have been upset about Cullen's lies. She just knew I couldn't stand him."

"It must have been hard on you," mused Myrtle, "that your wife, who has had so many health problems, needed the money so much more than your brother who wasted it."

"I thought the money was gone, or I would have found a way to get some of it a year ago," said Simon. "I thought that since Jill was working so hard that they must be totally out of cash. I didn't know about the lottery ticket."

"I suppose," said Myrtle thoughtfully, still watching the knife, "that it was an easy decision to kill Cullen. He'd double-crossed you, fixed it so you couldn't even talk to your father at the end of his life. He'd basically stolen the money from you—money you could have used to treat your wife's cancer. And, once you found out that Jill *did* have money and she was so conveniently murdered, all it took was for you to knock off Cullen and the money would finally be yours.

What I don't know," Myrtle continued, "is how you knew you were in Cullen's will. Why were you so sure he wouldn't send the money over to a far-flung relative or a charity or something?"

Simon snorted. "Cullen? Charitable? Please. Willow had mentioned before that Cullen was too lazy to even make out a will. She was worried about Jill being taken care of. She said that *Jill* had actually made a will and left everything to Cullen. And I'm Cullen's next of kin. It would have taken a while to work its way through probate court, but the money would have finally ended up where it needed to be."

Simon moved restlessly toward Myrtle and she babbled hurriedly. "So you put gloves on and went into your brother's house. You knew where he kept his gun because Jill has talked about it often enough. You made sure your fingerprints weren't on the gun at all and, of course, Cullen's would have been all over it."

Simon smirked. "Well, it *was* his gun."

"And you made it appear that he'd killed himself. You put his hand around it. Forced Cullen to pull the trigger. He must have been pretty drunk. That was quite a chance you took, wasn't it? What if you'd gotten there and he'd been completely sober?"

"I would have come back later. But I wasn't taking much of a chance, considering Cullen's pattern of drunkenness the last couple of days."

"But you made a mistake when you typed out a suicide note."

"As far as I knew, Cullen *had* killed Jill. And, I figured if he *hadn't*, nobody was going to come forward and correct the police and admit to the crime. It seemed like a good way to reinforce the fact that it was suicide."

"Except that Willow had already been arrested for Jill's murder and confessed to having done it."

"Except for that. Yes. But I had no way of knowing that Willow was going to be discovered the same night I killed Cullen. It was a *good* idea at the time." Simon sounded petulant.

Myrtle raised her eyebrows. He actually needed a pat on the back *that* badly? From someone he was going to murder?

"Jill had left him money. A significant *amount* of money."

Simon gave a short laugh. "And how long would *that* have lasted? Remember, he was drinking liquor all day long and had no income whatsoever. He would have burned through that money fast. And it would have been a total waste. How much better would it be to use that money to help Libba? And to maybe do some good for once?"

"Plus, you succeeded in making Cullen look weak. Weak enough to take his own life and as weak as you thought he made you look to your father." Myrtle pressed her lips into a thin line as Simon advanced with his knife. "There's nothing you're going to solve if you kill me. Now you're even using your own knife. You're going to lead Red right to you."

Simon said, "This knife? There's nothing special about it—except it came from Jill and Cullen's house. I thought it might come in handy one day, so I took it with me the other night. And murdering you *will* solve some problems for me. I'll have my freedom still and the money to enjoy it for the first time in my life."

And at that very moment, a miracle happened. From the corner of her eye, Myrtle glimpsed that the arrival of her savior, in the unlikely form of Pasha the feral cat. Pasha had crept through the open kitchen window (thank God for the burned biscuits) and was making one more determined effort to show Myrtle how to hunt and kill. Myrtle thanked her lucky stars. This time, she carried her most unusual prey yet—a live bat.

Simon, so focused on *his* prey, and still gabbing exultantly about getting away with murder, was completely unaware of Pasha's gift ... .until the bat, dumped on the floor by the cat, flapped awkwardly up and flew smack into Simon's head.

Simon looked stricken, eyes wide open, mouth agape and flapping as he dropped the knife to wave his arms frantically at the bat. Myrtle—a lot less worried about the bat than she was about Simon—picked up her cane in both hands and, with the new-found strength courtesy of fear and the new gym membership, cracked it over Simon's head.

He crashed to the floor in a heap and Myrtle quickly stooped and picked up the knife with shaking hands and backed up to the telephone to call Red. Pasha looked at the unconscious Simon curiously. She seemed impressed by the size of Myrtle's prey. And so ended Myrtle's hunting lessons from Pasha.

The police were also impressed with Myrtle's prey, who cooperatively remained unconscious until their arrival.

"I'm not sure why you keep opening the door to killers, Mama," said Red. "I'd have thought you'd have learned your lesson after Willow."

"I had no idea that Willow was a murderer until later in her visit, Red, as you well know."

"Okay, but you apparently knew that Simon killed Cullen. If you go around killing your own siblings, it's not likely that there's much in the way of morals holding you back from murdering snoopy old ladies."

"He forced his way in! And held a knife on me." said Myrtle. "What else was I supposed to do? I was planning on calling you right before he pushed into the house. I had no thoughts of confronting Simon Caulfield, I promise you."

Lieutenant Perkins quickly stepped in to prevent the spat going any farther. "Well, whatever you did, we owe you some gratitude, Mrs. Clover. Again. You've gotten a very dangerous man off the streets."

"Pasha was really the hero," said Myrtle, an uncharacteristic tear trickling out of her eye. She quickly wiped it away, frowning in irritation with herself. "Trying to share her bat with me. What a little love."

Detective Perkins could think of other descriptions of the cat that were a lot more apt. His guys had had a hell of a time capturing the cat *and* the bat. Since Mrs. Clover had mentioned that the cat needed its shots and to be spayed, they'd tracked it down and finally gotten the hissing, spitting creature into a cage to be taken to the vet. The bat had been easier, in comparison.

"It certainly looks as though Pasha deserves a medal," he said, soothingly. "I know how everything ended, but I'm not sure how you pegged Simon Caulfield for his brother's murder."

Myrtle beamed. She was always most pleased when being asked how she'd unraveled the case. "Simon was always a likely suspect. After all, I'd seen Cullen and Simon get into a fist fight at Fit Life. There was obviously a lot of old anger and resentment there."

"Not only did anger provide a motive, but when Puddin was cleaning my house the other day, she noted that Simon and Libba had fallen on hard times. That's something that was news to me. They'd never been wealthy people, but they'd always gotten by fairly well. But Puddin said that her cousin said that the Caulfields were even having trouble paying their grocery bill and had to let Puddin go as a cleaner. And Tiny Kirk said that he didn't think Simon was going to be able to pay him for the yard work at Cullen's house." Myrtle ignored Red's eye roll at the convoluted third-hand gossip.

"So Simon needed the money," said Lieutenant Perkins.

"He was Cullen's only living relative, so he knew the money would come his way at some point. And he knew that there *was* some money there because Georgia Simpson kept complaining about the lottery money she thought she'd been cheated out of."

"There was definitely a motive," said Red. "But how did you determine he was the killer?"

Myrtle looked discomfited. "From Kojak."

"Kojak!"

"Yes," said Myrtle with great irritation. "Don't look like that. I didn't have a long intellectual conversation with the dog or anything. But Willow had called me the morning after she'd tried to kill me."

Myrtle ignored the fact that Red was holding his head like it hurt. "She only wanted me to check on Kojak for her. She thought I was a big animal lover because of the Friends of Ferals thing. And maybe I am," said Myrtle, thinking gratefully again about Pasha's role in saving her life. "I suggested that maybe Kojak could have a home with Simon and Libba. Apparently, they'd already taken in the cat, Miss Chivis. But Willow was adamant that Kojak hated Simon. I guess the dog had witnessed too many scuffles between Cullen and his master's brother."

Perkins nodded encouragingly.

"But when I went over there, Kojak was really wailing. He sounded horrible. Sherry and I went in and discovered Cullen's body, which had been what upset the dog so badly."

"Then," Myrtle continued, "I went over to the Caulfields' house to bring some food over. Tippy had gotten me on that bereavement committee so Blanche and I went over to visit."

Red looked concerned. "Libba Caulfield ate your food, Mama?"

"And *loved* every bite," said Myrtle. She had no idea whether Libba had even eaten any of the casserole, but she was really getting quite fed up with these inferences.

"Anyway," said Myrtle, "Simon came in with shorts on and a huge bandage on his leg. Like something had tried to eat him."

Red frowned, "I don't think Cullen was in any shape to have fought Simon off, Mama."

"No, no! *Kojak* had bitten him. The dog had attacked Simon when he killed his master."

"And when I asked Simon how he'd gotten hurt, he said he'd been hurt while mowing his brother's grass. But I'd *seen* Tiny Kirk out there, mowing the grass, when I was looking after Kojak. I *knew* Simon had lied. And then, when I'd gotten back home, I heard dogs barking outside and I remembered poor Kojak."

Perkins and Red looked at each other again. Myrtle thought they looked tired.

"But Red, you'll be delighted to hear that I've got plans to do some quieter activities now."

Red raised his eyebrows.

"I'm going to write the most exciting story the *Bradley Bugle* readers have ever read. It's going to be the perfect follow-up to the story I wrote about Willow. And maybe," said Myrtle, "I'll even blog about it. You know—put some extra bits of information on the blog for the online readers."

Red put his head in his hands like he thought it might go spinning off. "Wait. You're exercising at the gym—-and working out enough to fend off a man over thirty years younger than you are. You've started going back to church. You managed to cook a casserole that apparently didn't kill Libba Caulfield (at least as far as we're aware.) And you're *blogging* too?"

Myrtle looked smug. "Social media is the new frontier." Myrtle wasn't exactly sure what social media *was*, but she loved the complete bewilderment on Red's face. The next week was going to be fun. Wait 'til she joined Twitter.

Acknowledgments: Thanks, as always, to my family for their love and support. Thanks to my mother, Beth Spann, a fabulous first reader. Thanks to Kendel Flaum for the lovely cover and Judy Beatty for her careful editing. And thanks to the online writing community, for all their help and encouragement.

About the Author:

Elizabeth writes the Southern Quilting mysteries and Memphis Barbeque mysteries for Penguin Random House and the Myrtle Clover series for Midnight Ink and independently. She blogs at ElizabethSpannCraig.com/blog , named by Writer's Digest as one of the 101 Best Websites for Writers. Elizabeth makes her home in Matthews, North Carolina, with her husband and two teenage children.

Other Works by the Author:

Myrtle Clover Series in Order:

Pretty is as Pretty Dies

Progressive Dinner Deadly

A Dyeing Shame

A Body in the Backyard

Death at a Drop-In

A Body at Book Club

Death Pays a Visit

A Body at Bunco

Murder on Opening Night

Cruising for Murder (2016)

Southern Quilting Mysteries in Order:

Quilt or Innocence

Knot What it Seams

Quilt Trip

Shear Trouble

Tying the Knot

Patch of Trouble (2016)

Memphis Barbeque Mysteries in Order (Written as Riley Adams):

Delicious and Suspicious
Finger Lickin' Dead
Hickory Smoked Homicide
Rubbed Out

And a standalone "cozy zombie" novel: Race to Refuge, written as Liz Craig

Where to Connect With Elizabeth:
Facebook: Elizabeth Spann Craig Author
Twitter: @elizabethscraig
Website: elizabethspanncraig.com
Email: mailto:elizabethspanncraig@gmail.com

Thanks!

Thanks so much for reading my book ... I appreciate it. If you enjoyed the story, would you please leave a short review on the site where you purchased it? Just a few words would be great. Not only do I feel encouraged reading them, but they also help other readers discover my books. Thank you!

Extras:

Interested in having a character named after you? In a Myrtle Clover tote bag? Or even just your name listed in the acknowledgments of a future book? Visit my Patreon page at https://www.patreon.com/elizabethspanncraig

Made in the USA
Lexington, KY
03 March 2017